Irish *Love* Stories

Best Wishes
Brendan Nolan

Also by Brendan Nolan

Phoenix Park a History and Guidebook

The Irish Companion

Barking Mad: Tales of Liars, Lovers, Loonies and Layabouts

Dublin Folk Tales

Wexford Folk Tales

Wicklow Folk Tales

The Little Book of Dublin

Urban Legends of Dublin

Irish *Love* Stories

Brendan Nolan

Fresh Appeal
Dublin

This is for you

First published in Ireland in 2016
Fresh Appeal
138 Esker Lawns,
Lucan,
Co Dublin,
Ireland
www.freshappeal.ie
tel: 00 353 (0)1 628 11 25
cover illustration Maeve Kelly

ISBN 978-0-9560810-1-8
Printed in Ireland by Naas Printing Ltd, Naas, Co Kildare

Contents

Acknowledgements

Thanks to Jenny McKenzie and Sharon Geoghegan for the loving attention given to these stories and to Karin Tscholl who suggested these stories be told in my own way.

Thanks to: Jacinta Kenny, Katy Clarke, Michael O'Byrne, Micaela Sauber and you.

Not forgetting the production crew of: Rita, Rory, Kevin, Alison, Sheila, Michelle, Rachel, Josh, Holly, Leo and Luci.

Introduction

For lovers, yesterday was divine. Today is almost unbearable happiness. Tomorrow a promise.

True, wonderful, heart-stopping love. The kind of rapture that stands between us and life itself. Lovers don't count time; for love has no end.

'I love you', says a whisper in the breeze. 'I will love you for a thousand years.'

Love springs where it's least expected, a wild flower met by a dusty track. Or a warm shadow on a path on a moonlit night.

Love begins with a single glance. Being in love means remembering little things for one another. When two become one. When you love, you love. There's no more to be said. Love needs no spoken language to be understood; but, true love is not for the faint-hearted, for there are those who would thwart the path of true love, as some of our stories will show.

It is often the outside world that tries to say how and when and to whom love should be granted, as if such a gift is in the power of mortals. When even Aengus, God of Love and Poetry in the time of the Tuatha de Danaan of mythological times, could not help falling helplessly in love with his night visitor, who can set confines to the hearts of mortals?

For falling in love is a moment, love is a lifetime. When you meet the love of your life, your heart will feel no pain, for you are complete. Aengus endures many days and nights of torment as he seeks the whereabouts of his one love: Caer.

Our stories hail from many times and places; all have love and Ireland in common. But love is universal and love is timeless.

Here is the story of a prince who has a lake moved from one place to another to suit his beloved's terms and conditions of marriage. There is a man blessed, or cursed, with a love spot on his manly chest that renders women demented with desire when exposed to it. He embarks on a perilous journey with his lover for a life of passion that leads to his eventful demise in a foreign land with echoes of Romeo and Juliet in his *denouement*.

There is the never-ending search of the warrior chieftain for his beloved wife, abducted by a jealous druid, though many years later he discovers his love child grown wild and living with the animals in the forest, tended to by a wild deer who leaves food for him every day. That son becomes a beloved poet and storyteller in his own manhood and the subject of a journey of love by a beautiful maiden come from across the sea to be with him, for all time.

Love can take many forms.

Two lovers become swans and fly away to be together, evermore. Those that hear them passing above fall down in a faint and awaken three days later as refreshed as if newly born to the world.

A bride is stolen by the sidhe, the fairies, on her wedding night for she neglected to keep watch for them, such was her eagerness for her married life.

Here too is a full detailing of potions and lures to attract and recognise the love of your life, always allowing that you are single yet, and available for love's contentment.

Names of future partners and lovers and spouses may be revealed in many ways. A man uses the trail of a graveyard snail across a plate to discover the initials of his intended wife; others use dead cats to lure their unsuspecting heart's desire to imbibe enchanted tea with them.

These pages teem with gods and mortals and fairyfolk and even ordinary folk.

Were they all by some miracle of the author's imagination to appear in the same place at the same time they would be of many backgrounds, times and locations.

Yet, they would all have one thing in common.

Love.

They would tell how a seed of love can become a tree of life.

New lovers become their own folklore.

They inspire all to fall in love over again. You need no reason to be in love. To enjoy.

And be.

Loved.

Brendan Nolan
www.brendannolan.ie

1

Dream of love

First light heralds a new dawn, a new day, a new life in love. Its soft flush slips across the shadowed floor, gently loosing night's mantle in the bedchamber of Aengus, God of Love and Poetry. In the corner of the room, furthest from the light, the singing girl falls silent.

Last night, Aengus felt a soft breeze caress his face on the opening of the oaken door. The girl's outline complemented the moonshadow. Her singing was soft and gentle. He lay back the better to hear this enchanting song, for it brought unquestioned peace to him. When it was done, she sang again this girl whom he had never seen before. Each song more beautiful than the one before.

Aengus feared she would disappear at the slightest intervention by him. Even so, when full light came she was gone and the room was silent.

He enquired of his guards whom she might be. But none could tell, none could say they had seen the girl. In his frustration, Aengus berated them for being asleep on duty.

Enquiries continued through the day, to no avail.

Night found him in early repose, willing the girl to revisit. His every thought was of her. He held his breath to hear her tread upon the stair.

Almost on cue, his enchantress appeared with soft voice and soothing lyric. All were different, all were new.

On succeeding nights she appeared, never speaking, never drawing closer. For all that, Aengus was alone once more in the chill morning light. He did not even know her name. He smiled like a lovestruck fool when sharing her description with others, though all shook their heads in perplexity.

None could say why she had chosen to visit Aengus. But visit she did, again and again, for nights, for weeks, for months.

Then, through one dreadful long night of silence, he remained alone, though he stared at the unmoving door until sight almost left his eyes.

From that day Aengus ceased eating; or drinking; he listened but fitfully to others. Physicians were called to attend him while he faded away. None could restore him to his normal self. The girl illuminated his inner darkness. That light was dimmed and so was his will to live. He was alone and bereft.

This happened in early spring.

On an autumn morning as brown leaves fell from trees and lay curled on the rutted roadways, his mother, the goddess Boann, arrived at the home of Aengus with the wisest and oldest doctor in the entire land. They were made welcome. Their every need was attended to in the dún or fort, where Aengus held court.

Examination of the patient was thorough and included all known causes of sickness and wasting away then known to healers.

Nonetheless, the physician found nothing physically wrong with Aengus. The top and tail of it, he said, was that all went amiss when the girl failed to materialise and Aengus became indolent in his ways and in his life.

All ills besetting Aengus would disappear when the girl was found, the doctor declared with certainty.

Easier said than done said those closest to the weakened Aengus, for they had already searched in vain for this elusive girl. She was a dream, most people said, that Aengus created to pass a restless night. She would never be found. Boann, growing more alarmed, sent her people to search every corner of the land. If her son said the girl was alive then they should return her to the side of Aengus.

All over the central plane of the land, high up on the slope of the hills, down in lonely valleys, along the banks of moorland streams they searched for the girl. Every cove and inlet of lake and sea was searched, each echoing cave carefully examined and probed.

A year passed with no success in finding the girl.

In desperation, Boann went to visit The Dagda. If any had the ability to find this girl then it was he who was the most powerful of the gods. He was her lover and father of their love child Aengus.

The Dagda, supreme being of the Tuatha Dé Danann, mythological rulers of Ireland, had loved Boann, who inconveniently was married to Nechtan.

On discovering Boann was with child, The Dagda caused the sun to stand still for nine months; so Aengus was conceived, carried, and born in one day.

The Dagda decreed that the girl must be located no matter how far his people had to travel or how long the journey might be, or what hardship might be met.

The girl must be found to please The Dagda and to avoid his wrath should she not be discovered before Aengus expired of love. Months passed before word came from the far side of the country, from Bodb Derg of Munster, that the girl had been found.

Messengers revealed the girl's name to be Caer. She and her companions were under a spell of an enemy of their house. Each Samhain, that is November the first, she and her friends were transformed into swans who rose from a Munster lake to fly away in pairs for a twelve month. They returned one year later to be restored to their earthly form. That transformation, in turn, lasted one year when they changed into swans again.

Days were few before the bewitched swans were to take off again from the surface of the lake, when this news arrived at the fort of Aengus. Caer would soon be gone, once more.

Aengus and his swiftest warriors and fastest horses made haste for the roads then were poor rutted thoroughfares that followed old animal tracks. They were barely wide enough for two cows to pass in some places, in others, branches from opposite sides reached out to touch both shoulders of a passerby.

The short cold days of winter were in the air when they arrived at the lake.

Near the water, in one place, they saw fifty young women of Caer's age, fifty more in another location and a similar number directly by the water's edge.

They stood in pairs, attached to one another by a silver chain of adornment.

One alone wore a gold necklace and it was towards her that Aengus walked, though he needed no outstanding embellishment to recognise her.

'You are Caer.'

'Yes,' she replied. Her spoken voice was as beautiful as the voice of song that filled enchanted nights in his bed chamber.

'I waited for you, I waited every night, You never came, never. Where did you go? Why?'

'I wanted to come to you with all my heart; but I am under a spell that kept me from your side.'

'Come with me now,' he said.

'I cannot, for tomorrow we fly away; but if you return to this place in one year's time I will leave with you and I will be your companion for all of my year in human form.'

Aengus agreed, for he would have agreed to anything to have Caer by his side. Afterwards, he wondered why he consented to such a proposal.

On the following day, pairs of young women entered the water and became fully fledged swans bobbing on the black water beneath the threatening sky of an early winter's day.

When all were in, they gathered pace, swifter and swifter, along the lake.

Each pair followed another until they rose from the rippled surface to form graceful sets. The air was a great blur of white. When all were safely aloft, they dipped away to their different destinies. They grew smaller to the watchers by the lake. In time, the sky was empty and bleak. All that was left was the lapping of lake water. Aengus and his companions turned for home; but with a lift to their step now after such a long period of despondency.

One year later, Aengus stood by the lakeside shifting his weight from one foot to another with impatience.

He watched silently as pairs of swans swooped to touch down on home water.

With so many swans of identical appearance moving about it was difficult for an observer to tell one from another. Nonetheless, Aengus stepped to the water's edge to the only white swan with a trace of gold across her breast.

Though he reached out to her, Caer said: 'We must wait. From tomorrow, we will be together. I have thought of nothing else this twelve month.'

Aengus replied: 'I will not wait a day nor a year to be with you. I am a god of the Tuatha Dé Danann. I have my own powers that will break the spell you are under.'

Many thought he meant to take Caer from the water by force of will. But Aengus surprised those who watched. With rapture on his face he himself stepped into the lake. His form sank down until it assumed a different shape. All who saw were astounded.

While the watchers stared he became a magnificent swan that moved to Caer's side. Each curled a long neck around the other. And were content.

All other swans left the lake two by two and assumed human form once more until there was left just one single pair on the lake.

Caer and Aengus. Aengus and Caer

When all were gone, they swam away, to rise into the air as one.

Those beneath their flight path said heavenly harp music floated down as they passed over.

Anyone who heard this sound fell away to sleep for three days and three nights to arise refreshed then and as new to the world as if born again.

To this day, people walking by lake shore or water's edge raise their head at the sound of a pair of approaching swans.

They watch and listen for Aengus and Caer.

Lovers, forever.

2

Girl in a riddle

Two people were on a quest for love, though it was the Gobán Saor and his son who were involved to begin with for the Gobán was intent on finding a clever wife for his slow son. He took the lad with him on the way to build a castle for the King of Munster.

They came to a house where they sought a seat by the fire for the night on their long journey. In that dwelling were two daughters one of whom the Gobán Saor thought might make a match for his only son.

The Gobán was a mason and a storyteller and married to a woman that was a match for him in gentle deception. Between them, they produced a clutch of daughters. While he loved them all, none could become a builder, according to custom. In the end, a final child was born while the father was away. It was a daughter.

Anticipating her husband's disappointment, the Gobán's wife swapped babies with a neighbour who had given birth to a boy on the same day and who was moving away, shortly thereafter.

The neighbour took the girl child with her. She left her boy child behind, for she was pleased to have a girl child in the household, though afterwards she was pleased to bear a second girl, almost as a blessing, it seemed.

To the keen-eyed Gobán the infant presented to him was not of his flesh. Nonetheless, he pretended to be deceived and reared the child as his own.

As he grew, it seemed a poor swop was made for it took the boy two days to understand two minutes of instruction.

The only hope was to find a clever wife for him who would make up for his shortcomings. So the Gobán made a slight detour on their work journey to visit this house.

Studying the two young women in their seats in the company around the fire the Gobán observed that the older daughter with the long black shining hair was industrious but quiet about it, she mended a sock while she listened to all that was said. Her younger sibling had a fair complexion sure to attract the interest of many a young man fired up with nature's heat in his loins. This girl sat with her hands folded across her lap, and listened to the talk round the fire, the better to be noticed by anyone who came calling. She had little liking for any work that did not impress a suitor, it seemed.

The Gobán Saor told stories to the gathering from his time constructing forts for the great chiefs of Ireland. When he wanted to drive big nails into beams that were high up from the ground, he would pitch them into place with his hands. He'd take a fling of the hammer upwards at their heads, to drive them in as firm as you'd like. He would catch the hammer when it fell down once more, in case it landed on the head of any young lady sitting before the fire.

The fair-haired girl looked up at the ceiling lest anything might come tumbling down on her from that point. Her sister only smiled into the fire.

While they were chatting about one thing and another, the Gobán expressed a wish to be young once more; but if he did, he said, it was for the sake of securing one of them for a wife, though happily he was married to the mother of his son, now present at the fireside, and not available.

Having told them so, he wished them much success in their eventual choice of a husband. To while away the time until his return, he set them three pieces of a riddle.

The first was how to always to have the head of an old woman by the hob.

How to always warm yourself with work in the morning, was the second piece of the conundrum.

And, finally, some time before he and his son came back, they should take the skin of a newly-killed sheep to the market, and bring it and the price of it home again.

This mystified the sisters who pressed for more guidance, to no avail, for a riddle must not be explained, or else it would not be a riddle.

And when light and dark balanced each other at dawn they were prepared for the journey, awaiting only the sound of the cockcrow to be away.

To test his feelings the Gobán said to his son that perhaps one of the girls might be his wife some day, a prospect that pleased the son. And on they journeyed.

The King of Munster wanted a castle built that would show how powerful he was and belittle the castles and forts of his rivals. However, the king was in the habit of killing the craftsmen he employed to build his fortifications, so they would never build another palace equal to his.

Knowing so, the Gobán discussed the danger with his wife before acceptance of the commission. Together, they agreed a stratagem should peril present itself. When they came to where the King of Munster kept court, the Gobán and his son and their many assistants set to work. It was not long before great strides were made in the work.

While he worked, the son tried to put out of his mind the sisters back in the house, though the dark-haired girl was his favourite. He smiled often and loudly at her name when he recalled it. Rosín. Her sister Fiona's name hardly interfered with his work at all.

While the son was wandering about with a slower air than usual even for him, a worker came late one night to the Gobán. He said that just as they were setting the coping stone to finish the work, the scaffolding was set to become loose. The Gobán would fall to his death.

The king was planning to shed some tears, for the likes of this great builder would never be seen again, his highness would declaim.

The Gobán informed the king that he was nearly at the end; yet there was a small task to be completed before the wall-plate was made sure and strong. Sadly, the instrument to do that was at home, for he had quite forgotten to bring it with him.

He told the king that his wife would entrust it to no one not of royal blood. To that end, he said he would have to return home to fetch it in person, while his son remained to tidy up all else.

The king, rather than let the Gobán out of his sight, and caring little for his doltish offspring sent his own son, the young prince to fetch whatever was required. An outlandish name for the suposed tool had been agreed in advance by the Gobán with his wife, as a sign that treachery was afoot. He bade the king's son to make all haste, so the great castle could be finished.

In due course, the prince's attendants returned to say that while the king's son was safe and well he was detained against the safe return of the Gobán and his son.

So, the Gobán safely put the finishing touch to the palace in three days, and, in two days more, he and his son were sitting at the farmer's fireside where the two daughters of the house awaited their return.

For now the Gobán Saor was more interested in the response to the mystery he had set for the young women than the treachery of a greedy king.

He asked fair-haired Fiona if she remembered the riddle? She did and she reported she had taken an old woman's skull from the churchyard, and fixed it to the wall near the hob. However, it so frightened every one that came upon it she was obliged to have it taken back within an hour.

As to warming herself with work: the first morning's occupation was to card flax. She threw some of it onto the fire, thinking to warm herself. Her mother gave her such a raking for it, that she did not dare to warm herself that way again.

As for the sheepskin. When she told the buyers in the market that she was to bring back the skin and the price of it they mocked her, and so she left it with them without receiving payment for it at all.

So that was that for the fair-haired daughter.

The Gobán asked dark-haired Rosín how she fared? For the skull she persuaded an old woman to sit close to the fire tapping the side of her poor head, all the while.

As for warming herself in the cold mornings, she kept her hands and feet going so lively at her work that it was warming enough. The matter of the sheepskin was easy enough, laughed the girl, while the lovestruck son of the Gobán stared at her with his bottom jaw a little too far away from its upper twin for his father's comfort.

Arrived at the market with the sheepskin, she went to the crane, plucked the wool off, sold it, and brought home the skin.

Recognising straightaway the treasure he had met in this house, the Gobán asked the father and mother to give this girl to him as his daughter-in-law.

They were agreeable to the proposal. Rosín was agreeable to being his daughter-in-law, whatever about marrying the son. She recognised an idiot when she saw one; but was happy to adventure with the Gobán Saor for she knew she was almost a match for him in wit.

The wedding took place amid great merriment. The storytelling and enjoyment was so mighty that the newly-released prince, the son of the King of Munster, altered his route home to join the happy congregation. He and his friends danced their fine shoes off, almost.

He had enjoyed the company of the daughters of the Gobán Saor while in delightful captivity and was in no hurry to meet his stern and discommoded father.

As for the king, well he had his new cold castle in which to take comfort.

The wife of the Gobán Saor was content for she knew that her new daughter-in-law was her own forsaken child happily returned to her so many years later, and now back in her rightful family once more.

3

Fairy dancer

The sidhe have many ways of abducting humans. Sometimes it is by sweeping raid, other times by guile, charm and the fine steps of a dancer.

Kathleen was unaware of her fate when she stepped out to fetch water in the kitchen pail. It was dark and she expected to be back soon. She was the prettiest girl for many a mile, used to being interrupted in daylight by local youths intent on practicing their incipient seduction on her. Young men argued about her beauty; some said her dark shoulder-length hair was her attraction; some said her smile and white teeth far outshone any other woman within many days walking. More plumped for the softness of her lips, or, her dancing brown eyes, or the way she never showed impatience no matter how silly the conversation might be, for it was often the conversation was meant only to delay her while she was admired.

On this November night, she held the good white pail lightly in her white fingers. The well was not far away. She knew every childhood incline and declivity of the path. Kathleen hurried along, for the night was cold and her feet bare. She pulled her woollen shawl tighter. She meant to lean over to scoop water into the pail and be off home again.

For all her good intention, someone had splashed water on the ground earlier and by now it was a light skim of ice. Filled, Kathleen hefted the heavy bucket of water in both hands to stop it slapping out too much precious liquid.

Though she was sure-footed, she fell on the ice , something that had not happened in a very long time.

In falling she hit her head. It was sore where she touched it with the tip of her finger; but for now she was more concerned that her familiar surroundings had faded from her ken.

Open countryside replaced familiar houses and street while flames of a bonfire danced towards the sky a little distance away.

Kathleen left the fallen pail where it lay and walked hesitatingly across damp grass towards the forms around the fire. Stare as she might, she could see no face familiar to her though the people around her were neither younger nor older than herself.

The circle opened enough for her to stand shoulder to shoulder with the attendance. They were all striking-looking individuals with not a blemish between them. One she saw was more handsome than the others. This man stepped to her: 'I am Manus. You are very welcome. Kathleen.'

The sudden heat of the fire on a cold night and the closeness of this man who had eyes only for her made Kathleen almost faint away.

'Thank you,' she answered softly. 'But where is this? I don't remember being here before. Or, even seeing you.' She stopped then for a little breath for she was concerned that if she did not breathe soon she would fall down at his feet, with nobody of this company able to say where she lived so as to bring her home safely. A golden band pulled his long yellow hair back from his fine forehead. Kathleen thought he was beautiful, like a prince, with a red sash around his slim waist.

Then, he asked her to dance.

She thought he was teasing her, for there were no musicians here that she could see. No music sounded. Kathleen gazed into his blues eyes with bewitched abandon. He said nothing; but waited politely for response.

'I would dance with you; but there is no music .'

Manus raised a hand blessed with long smooth fingers that tapered into delicate nails more fitted for a maiden. The most delightful intoxicating music floated through the air. A piper and a fiddler a distance away played with heads bowed in reverence to their task.

Manus inclined his head. Kathleen placed her hand in his as if they had been partners forever.

There was a dancing place, a square worn down to hardness by the feet of many generations of these people she had fallen in with, whoever they were. How very strange that she had never seen any of them before.

The circle re-assembled around them. Sets formed of four dancers apiece. And they were away to the music, dancing their hearts out beneath a clear November sky.

It was no longer cold, in fact Kathleen felt the very opposite. She flung her shawl away and cared not where it landed though she could not afford to replace it if she could not find it when the dance was done.

Her feet danced in time to the strange music, her hair flying when she leaned back. Manus spun her around the dancing area, faster and faster.

Everywhere she looked there were dancers. Everyone flew around, laughing as they went. Kathleen sneaked a glance at Manus to see how he was doing and what he thought of her dancing. Manus smiled down at her and her heart skipped a beat. Kathleen knew she was a fine dancer, for men young and old waited their turn with her when the dance was held in the long room of their house.

The fire had been big enough to attract attention before it subsided into these glowing embers. The music was loud enough to hear across several townlands. And the laughter of her companions was so infectious she was sure the whole world could hear. Even so, there were no local people here.

They danced without lull or pause. It seemed the weaving dancers were used to this frenetic pace, for not one of them broke step, not once.

Nonetheless, no matter how long a November night may be it must yield to the small blue light of dawn when the human world resumes its business.

Both dancers and musicians were aware of the dawning of the day. For at a warning rasp of the fiddler's bow the piper made an end to the music and all was silent. All dancing stopped. All milled about among the crowd.

Manus took her hand. They stepped away from the fire and from the dancing floor. Kathleen walked languidly along with Manus by her side. The quietened dancers walked along behind them.

Before long, they came to a hollow in the ground. Kathleen had never seen this place before. A door in the grass opened wide to the night. A trapdoor, steps led down to a lower chamber. Kathleen did not hesitate when Manus led her down to what was a well-lit high-vaulted room.

If the night outside had been dark, here everything was bright and shining with hundreds of candles in angled holders arrayed along the walls.

Long wooden tables were burdened with an abundance of food and drink that an impoverished Kathleen had never seen before. That they were arrayed in vessels of gold and silver seemed perfectly normal, on this night.

She was not surprised to see that Manus had a high-backed chair to himself, or, that she was seated in a similar chair beside him.

Overcome somewhat by the glory of it all, Kathleen hesitated to take anything until she quietly observed the behaviour of others.

Then, she took a golden cup that Manus handed to her. She raised it to her parched lips to drink.

But, a man she did not know manouevered himself around to the back of her seat, and whispered that she was not to eat any food, nor drink any wine, or she would never reach her mortal home again. He looked familiar, like someone she met in a dream of long ago.

Kathleen lay down the cup, and declined to drink. She would not accept the food Manus brought to her lips on the end of his bejewelled knife.

Seeing this, her fellow diners became angry, and a great noise arose in the room, far louder than any she heard when the dancing and music had been at its height by the fire.

One fierce dark man stood and said that whoever came to them must drink and eat with them. So saying, he seized Kathleen's arm. He held the cup to her lips. Manus was pushed aside; but made no move to recover the situation for her.

By now frightened and wondering what to do or how to escape Kathleen thought the worst when a red-haired man took her by the hand to lead her out all the while making way for her with his other arm as they went.

Once outside, he entrusted her with a branch of ground ivy by the name of Athair-Luss. If Kathleen held it in her hand until she reached home, no one could harm her, he whispered in fierce and urgent tone.

Thoroughly frightened by now, Kathleen ran up the steps and along the dew damp grass as fast as her dance-tingling feet would allow, all the time fancying she heard hurrying footsteps closing on her.

With gasping breath, Kathleen reached home and barred the door, and went to bed, even though it was almost full daylight, though she could not sleep.

A clamour arose outside when hurrying voices arrived at her abode.

Voices cried to her that when next she danced to the music by the fire, she would stay with them and no one would deny that.

In time, the voices faded away to a few single mutterings and all was quiet outside. Kathleen kept the ivy with her through her life and was never bothered by any one again on any night by the well, though she remained ever vigilant.

However, it was long and long before the sound of the fairy music left her ears that she had danced to that November night by the dancing fire with Manus, her fairy lover.

It was never to be that Manus left her imagination or consciousness in the long years until her own breath left her and she was found with a smile on her lips.

4

Dance of love

It is not only ordinary girls who have adventures in the dark of night when going to draw water for the household for there is a story of a king's daughter who caused a great phenomenon to occur when she performed a similar task.

It was neither her idea or choice to leave the company to fetch water for that was the work of a serving girl, but the circumstances were far from ordinary.

A great king who was known as King Core had a palace in a glen along which the usual rivers and streams would be supposed to have flown. It was in a round green valley, in the Cork area of the country, according to T Crofton Croker a 19th century collector of stories who many years later was reminded of what happened by oral storytellers of the time.

In the middle of the courtyard of the palace was a spring of fair water, so pure, and so clear, that it was the wonder of all who tasted it or who heard tell of it. The king of course rejoiced at having so great a curiosity within his palace; but being mortal he also feared the well would run dry as people came in crowds from far and near to draw the precious water of this spring. He was sorely afraid that in time it might indeed become dry.

King Core caused a high wall to be built up around it. Into this wall was inserted a heavy wooden door. He would allow nobody to have the water except for his own household. This was a very great loss to the poor people living about the palace, who had to throw wooden buckets into the river on hemp ropes to drag in whatever water they needed.

Further, whenever the king wanted pure water for himself, he would send his daughter to fetch it, not trusting his servants with the key of the well-door, fearing they might give some away.

This of course did not best please his daughter, but being dutiful she obeyed her father's wishes. Then one fateful night the king gave a grand entertainment to which came many great princes present, and lords and nobles.

There seemed to be no end to the finery.

To please the multitude there were jugglers and tumblers aplenty many of them performing well rehearsed feats that seemed to the amazed audience to be the first time the feat was ever performed.

There were wonderful doings throughout the palace: there were bonfires, whose red and yellow flying sparks blazed up to the very sky; dancing was there to such sweet music, that it ought to have woken the dead out of their graves or the fairies from their watching forts.

There was feasting that few could remember in its magnificence. There was the greatest of plenty for all who came. No one was turned away from the palace gates.

The guardians of the gate were instructed to say to everyone: 'You're welcome - you're welcome, heartily.'

It was the porter's salute for all.

Many manly princes came with the thought of speaking soft words into the kind ear of the king's daughter. Many rehearsed their words haltingly until they were word perfect when they arrived in a throng with others intent on the same pursuit.

But, while she listened to all and compared them in her mind with one another there was one alone who was outstanding in her eyes.

For it happened at this grand entertainment that one young prince stood above all the rest. He was mighty comely to behold, and as tall and as straight as ever eye would wish to look on. Right merrily did he dance that night with the old king's daughter, wheeling here, and wheeling there, as light as a feather, and footing it away to the admiration of every one. The musicians played the better for seeing their steps; and the pair danced as if their lives depended upon it. They went on almost to exhaustion.

After all this dancing came the supper when the young prince was seated at table by the side of his beautiful partner, who smiled upon him as often as he spoke to her.

That was by no means as often as he wished, for he had to turn constantly to the company and thank them for the many compliments passed upon his fair partner and himself, when all he and the princess wanted was to be alone with one another.

It seemed they were set fair for a time of happiness together. But who could foretell what was to happen over a simple thing like a drought of water for the table and the request of a father to a daughter?

In the midst of this overflowing banquet, one of the great lords said to King Core: 'May it please your majesty, here is every thing in abundance that heart can wish for, both to eat and drink, except water.'

This want the king had arranged so he could meet the call and show off his wonderful daughter to the company while doing so.

'Water !' said the king, mightily pleased at someone calling for that of which purposely there was a want: 'water shall you have, my lord, speedily, and that of such a delicious kind, that I challenge all the world to equal it.'

Turning to his daughter, he said in a very loud and important voice: 'Daughter, go fetch some in the golden vessel which I caused to be made for the purpose.'

The king's daughter, who was called Fior Usga, which is an old spelling of Fior Uisce or Spring Water in English, did not much like to be told to perform so menial a service before so many people, and though she did not dare refuse a command of her father, she hesitated to obey him, and looked down upon the ground in mild distress.

The king, who loved his daughter very much, seeing this, was sorry for what he had desired her to do, but having said the word, he was never known to recall it; he therefore thought of a way to persuade his daughter go speedily and fetch the water.

The solution was simple yet complex. The king proposed that the young prince should partner her along the way as he had done in dancing. It was a fine solution in the opinion of the princess.

Accordingly, with a loud voice, he said: 'Daughter, I wonder not at your fearing to go alone so late at night; but I doubt not the young prince at your side will go with you.'

The prince was very much not displeased at hearing this; and taking the golden vessel in one hand, with the other he led the king's daughter out of the hall so gracefully that all present gazed after them with delight.

When they came to the spring of water, in the court-yard of the palace, the fair Usga unlocked the door with the greatest care, and smiled at her companion.

She stooped down with the golden vessel to take some water from the well. She scooped well and deep the better to impress her partner with her skill; but since there is many a slip between cup and lip she found the vessel so heavy that she lost her balance and fell into the well, sinking down immediately.

The young prince tried in vain to save her, for the water rose and rose so fast, that the entire court-yard was speedily covered with it, and he hastened back in a state of distraction to the king and the company seeking assistance.

The door of the well being left open, the water, which had been so long confined, rushed forth incessantly, every moment rising higher and higher, and was in the great hall of entertainment sooner than the young prince himself.

When he attempted to speak to the king he was up to his neck in water. It rose to such a height that it filled the entire green valley in which the king's palace stood, and so a full lough was formed where none had been ever before in anyone's memory.

Yet, magically, the king and his guests were not drowned; neither was his daughter, the fair Usga, who returned to the banquet hall the very next night after this dreadful event.

Every night since then the same entertainment and dancing goes on in the palace at the bottom of the lough, and will last until someone brings up out of it the golden vessel which was the cause of all this mischief.

Nobody can doubt that it was a judgment upon the king for his shutting up the well in the courtyard from the poor people.

And when the waters of the lough are low and clear, the tops of towers and stately buildings may be plainly viewed in the bottom by those who have good eyesight, if they have a mind to peer into the depths.

They may even see the king's daughter and her prince dance there forever in the dance of love.

5

Met upon the road

Many stories are told of ill-fated lovers whose destiny it is never to see their love fulfilled. Baillé and Aillinn were two such lovers though they were united in an unexpected way, many years later.

The Ulster prince Baillé was the sweet-tongued son of Buan. He was infatuated with the lovely Leinster princess, Aillinn, daughter of Lucha, and Lughaidh.

They arranged to meet at Ros na Righ, a place that lay equal distance from both. In the meantime, they despatched earnest declarations of true love.

Baillé was first to make ready with his retinue of trusted escorts. They waited only for the cock to crow away the darkness of night. Rush lights flickered in the fading shadows. Colourful cloaks draped manly shoulders. Horses were saddled, pack animals checked, defensive weapons secured, and food taken in preparation for the day. A band of happy musicians went along to lighten the journey.

And so they proceeded. They had arrived as far as the coast by Dundealgin when their destiny was changed, forever.

Baillé was comfortably riding along in the sunlight on his favourite horse on his chosen saddle, reins held lightly in his hands looking forward to this happy encounter when he noticed a hurrying man, a stranger not of their company, approaching with some intent.

Like the darting of a hawk down a cliff, or a strong wind from off the sea, the tall and wild-looking stranger closed the gap between them with every stride. Though the intruder was upon the prince before any could come between them, he failed to lay hands upon Baillé.

The man was unarmed and stood in sullen silence .

Civilly enough, Baillé asked him his purpose. 'Where have you travelled from and whither go you in such a flurry? Why have you he presumed to approach a prince in such a manner? You are lucky be alive such is your insolence.'

'I have come from Mount Leinster, away to the south and was proceeding northwards to the River Bann, where I was born. On this day I do not bring pleasant news,' the man replied in a surprisingly level tone for one who had arrived in such a scattering of time.

He said: 'Princess Aillinn set out from Dun-Righ, without her father's approval, to meet Prince Baillé at the Boyne, which is not far distant from where we are halted. But, there is an old prophecy that says Prince Baillé and Princess Aillinn will never meet.'

He went on to say that the men of Leinster overtook the princess and her entourage on the road and detained her. They would prevent her going any farther, until her father decreed otherwise.

Yet, so much was her soul set on meeting Baillé that within an hour of her detention and denial of such a meeting, mortal life left her young body in complete and total sorrow, the horrified company heard the stranger say.

All fell silent.

They were further disturbed moments later when the messenger vanished from among them as a fairy wind might whip across green summer grass.

Baillé was seen to cry out at the news. All who heard feared for his sanity. Those closest to him rushed forward but Baillé slipped from his horse to the ground, it seemed, in a faint, though it was to prove to be the faint of death.

For the prince's heart had burst at the news. In the moment, breaking waves ceased to sound, sea birds did not call or wheel through the blue air. Many in the entourage wept openly.

With all life departed from within it seemed fitting to his friends to bury their leader where he fell on his journey, between what had been and what was to be.

So, Baillé was interred by the sea, with great ululation. It came as little surprise to his mourners that in no time at all a yew tree sprang up from his grave in a much shorter span than nature ever demanded for such alchemy.

The days following were a great sorrow to all who knew the young prince and his ready smile. However, a falsehood had been perpetrated by Otherworld forces intent on denying these young lovers union and happiness, in payment for some ancient but unforgotten wrong from a time before either were even conceived.

For, while Baillé was hearing the fatal and fraudulent news, a very much alive Aillinn was making preparations for the journey north. Her chamber faced the sun's journey across the sky and made for a happy room, though one she was content to leave to live with Baillé in a home of their own.

Looking forward to peace and happiness and love Aillinn was heart-startled when the same fierce-looking individual as had appeared before Baillé materialised before her. She made to call for her guards; but his terrible demeanour made her hesitate.

He had ragged long straw-coloured hair; his squirrel eyes in a skinny face missed nothing. He had been at Dundealgin, he declared, where men he saw piling up a cairn of stones over a newly filled-in grave. Each placed their own tribute on the heap of rocks, he said. They inscribed, with ogham marks on an upright stone, how Baillé Mac Buan died on that spot as he was proceeding to meet the fair Aillinn daughter of Lucha, and Lughaidh. With that, the strange man vanished. Though if he had retired gracefully from the room, Aillinn would not have noticed his going.

For she too fell lifeless to the floor. Her young life left her, in heartfelt anguish.

Hearing a cry and a falling sound her people found her curled up on the wooden floor when they came to her. Try as they might, they could do nothing to recall the departed soul to its earthly body. Aillinn was no more, her bright flower was withered and gone.

Her remains were buried amid widespread lamentation. Before long a beautiful apple tree sprang from her grave to the astonishment of all.

There the tragedy might have lain, lost to all but storytellers and poets and ballad makers as a tragedy of young love denied. Except, that at the end of seven years, the actions of others was to bring Baillé and Aillinn together once more.

Some poets, prophets, and seers of Ulster, cut down the yew tree that stood over the grave of Baillé, and made its wood into a Tabhall Filidh or Poet's Tablet.

It was on this tablet that poets wrote of the visions, espousals, loves, and courtships of Ulster across many years.

Others felled the apple tree over the grave of Aillinn. On this was written the courtships, loves, and espousals, of Leinster.

And there the story waited. The lovers resting places were not otherwise disturbed. Though no replacement tree grew on either grave.

A long time afterwards, 200 years later, in the second century of Our Lord, at the great feast of Samhain that marked the end of summer and the beginning of winter from November the first onwards, poets and practitioners of arts all came to Tara, the seat of the High King of Ireland.

As was the custom, they brought their tablets to write upon, and to display. Many tried to impress their rivals with the wonder of their individual tablet.

Among the many such tablets were two, one was made of Ulster yew, the other of Leinster applewood.

King Art, the mightiest king in the land held each of them in his hands, face to face. He reflected on the old story that the lovers would never meet.

With great interest, he traced the lines of the weathered woods with his calloused and battle hardened fingers while their respective owners awaited the return of their tablets with a mixture of pride and anxiety.

If the death of Baillé and the sudden demise of Aillinn on the same day had shocked all those present at the time, then their descendents were shocked in turn when each wooden tablet eagerly sprang to the other, in Art's hands, though he tried to hold them as steadily as he could

Each became bound to the other as the sweet woodbine binds itself to the green branch.

Once joined, neither tablet would separate from the other, try as the strongest among them might, for they were united at last.

For if it was foretold by druids and prophets that Aillinn and Baillé would not marry. It was also foretold that they would meet after their deaths, and once met, would never part again.

6

Recovered bride

Any couple joining in wedlock when fairies are raiding the world of humans dances with danger. For the intruders will sweep the bride away in a moment. Such a raid occurred in Curragraigue, when Maggie was preparing for her wedding night on the happiest day in late spring.

For the ceremony, Maggie wore her bridal hair in braids with ribbon and lace woven through the plaits. Her blue wedding dress symbolised purity.

Thomas wore his best trousers and a fine white shirt, though his feet felt awkward in the new boots for he spent his days on the land barefoot and his toes did not fully understand what was required of them in boots.

In the moment, Thomas's right hand held Maggie's right hand, each left hand joined the other's left hand, their wrists crossed. A ribbon wound around their wrists over the top of one and under and around the other, creating their own symbol of infinity.

And they were wed.

The feasting and celebration began after a foot race by all to the cottage won of course by the bride, as it should be. There was dancing and singing and eating and drinking. Storytelling and lie telling and boasting and ribald advice to the groom were offered up in great merriment.

When the evening was done, the remaining guests prepared for making noise outside the window of the bridal room to speed the marriage along, and to wish the new couple well.

Maggie stepped into their newly painted bedroom to prepare herself.

Thomas chatted nervously to his friends for a moment. As casually as he could, he took his leave to step to the closed door of the room. Gingerly, he opened the door and stepped inside.

But, the remaining guests were soon startled by the groom rushing back into the room with anguish and torment on his young face.

When he could speak, after many attempts to do so, he said: 'Maggie is carried away by the sidhe. There is no more sign of her there than if she never was born.'

There was only one door into that bedroom. The window was small. It had not been opened in many years. It was closed still. Maggie had vanished from the face of the Earth.

Astonished guests rose or turned to others where they were standing. Those enjoying a pipe outside came in from the cool night to declare that nobody had passed them.

Others thought perhaps Thomas was playing a joke, for he was well known for teasing people with tall stories. Perhaps, he was having a final moment of fun? However, one look at his stricken face was enough to show he was in earnest.

The ripples of a search spread away into the night. They began in the house; they moved into the yard; they visited all the newly white-washed outbuildings.

Maggie was not there. It was as if she had never lived among them. They searched and searched for her. Those that knew the way of the sidhe shook their heads in sadness. Maggie was gone with the fairies, the sidhe. In time and time, grey dawn flecked the empty sky.

Wedding guests wandered here and there in case they had missed a sign. And when light came to the countryside once more with new dawn, all searched again on the day that should have been the couple's first day together. In vain.

Some had to go home for they had livestock to tend; interrupted lives to resume once more. After a night and a further day spent in misery, Thomas, the poor bridegroom, lay down to take some rest, on his bridal bed. Alone.

He left the door to the main room open so he could watch the falling shadows from the quietening fire.

He drew some comfort from their familiarity. Moonlight that spilled in to the next room mesmerised and seduced him to drowsiness.

It seemed to him then that he awoke from a troubled dream. He looked out into the room once more. In the middle of the slanting rays of the moon stood his Maggie in her light blue bridal clothes.

He tried and tried but found his tongue was without utterance, no words would pass his lips; his limbs were unable to move.

'Do not be disturbed, dear husband,' said the form. Her voice was as pure as her shy spoken vows, just one day before.

She was in the power of the fairies, the sidhe. She told a terrified Thomas that if he only had courage they might be soon happy again.

The following Friday would be Mayeve, and the entire fairy court would ride out of the old fairy fort after midnight, to greet the first day of summer. Mayday.

Maggie said she would be there in the midst of it all, on horseback.

'You must sprinkle a circle with holy water, and have a black-hafted knife with you,' she explained. 'If you can pull me off the horse and draw me into the ring with you, all they can do will be useless.'

Thomas nodded his head, for he could not speak.

'You must leave some food every night on the dresser in the kitchen, for if I taste one mouthful with them, I will be lost to you for ever.' said Maggie.

Thomas struggled to rise to find some currant bread for her before he realised it was of nights yet to come she spoke. Without words he asked her what happened?

She answered: 'The sidhe got power over me because I was only thinking of you on our wedding day, such is my love for you. I did not prepare myself as I ought to by being vigilant against the malevolence of the sidhe.'

Thomas cried out and struggled from the bed; but was too late for one movement caused another and Maggie vanished before he could reach her.

Each evening Thomas made sure food was left on the dresser. Each morning, it was gone.

Emboldened by the certainty that Maggie was helping him, Thomas stationed himself at the entrance of the old rath, the fort, a little before midnight on Mayeve.

He formed the circle on the ground from a small whiskey bottle filled with holy water from a barrel behind the church.

He held the knife in his hand with determination, and trepidation.

He alternated between fear of losing his dear Maggie to the sidhe, forever, and burning with impatience for the confrontation to come.

He knew the old fort all of his life. In truth it was a low wall encircling a space with green grass growing over all. He knew the stories, as everyone did, of this being a fort of the sidhe and that mortals should keep away. But now it became a real palace complete with its own court before his eyes.

Light from many candles spilled from the windows and out of the high entrance hall. Rush torches were held aloft by small people stationed around the courtyard, throwing illumination into shadow.

Thomas drew breath as a cavalcade of richly-attired men and women of the sidhe moved towards the gateway, where he awaited them.

They rode by him laughing and jesting. He felt they should see him; but he could not tell whether they were aware of his presence or not.

He looked intently at each as they approached, but he could not see Maggie anywhere.

Then he saw her mounted on a milk-white horse riding on a fine Spanish saddle on the far side of the crowd. The press of the crowd meant she could not get close enough to Thomas to be rescued by him.

Maggie saw him. Across her features swept a smile of happiness. It was accompanied by deep anxiety at the peril she was in unless she moved closer to Thomas.

Throwing his own safety aside, Thomas rushed out of the holy circle away from his own safety.

He swam through the mass of protesting horseflesh. He pushed and shoved his way to Maggie's side. He slashed through the rein with the black hafted knife. Reaching up, Thomas seized his bride in his arms, and lifted her from the horse.

Cries of rage and fury arose on every side from the sidhe as they realised a demonic human was among them stealing back his bride.

Thomas and Maggie were hemmed in on all sides. Weapons were directed at his head and body to terrify him. But Thomas responded by wielding the black-hafted knife Maggie had urged him to bring with him.

The sidhe seemed confused by his counter threat of using the knife against them and fell back.

Holding Maggie by her agreeable waist, Thomas moved towards the blessed circle. Soon, they stood inside it, hands joined just as they had held hands on their wedding day.

Maggie and Thomas breathed together, daring to believe they were free of the sidhe.

They waited until bodies and horses were carried away by the moving procession and lights faded from the fort to leave but overgrown walls once more.

When it was safe, they stepped along the road to their home, holding hands.

They saw the light from their own kitchen spilling into the farmyard in welcome.

They smiled.

Together.

7

Children of the dead woman

It was often that a man lost his wife long ago in Ireland for times were hard on everyone.

There was a man who was only a year married when his good wife died, while giving birth to their child. The child was hale and hearty but the woman lay on the bed without movement at all. It was decided that she was dead and the remains were buried.

The man decided he would try to rear the child himself with the assistance of an old neighbour woman who hired out for that class of engagement.

The woman moved in to his house to sleep in a bed beside the fire with the cradle nearby, so she could attend to the child by night and by day. All was fine for a pair of months until the father complimented the old woman on the health of the child and her care of him, on one stormy night when he came in from the night and his work outside.

However, the carer told him it was not she who was responsible for the health of the child but its own mother.

She related to the startled husband that every night the mother came in to eat some boiled potatoes and drink some milk from the cupboard. She warmed her hands at the fire and went to the cradle and kissed the child and fed him at her breast. She washed him then, put dry clothes under him, and lay him down in the cradle, kissing him again.

She stood on the floor then, looked up toward the room where her husband slept, sighed, and left. This she did every night, said the old woman.

The surprised husband declared that had he known that she was in his house every night he would have held her here. To which the old woman replied that she would cough when his wife came in that night and he could make his attempts to detain her.

He lay that night on the bed with most of his clothes on him so he would see his wife and could move to detain her.

In due course, the child's mother arrived in. She went to the cupboard and ate quickly, and steadily, washing the potatoes down with fresh milk. She stirred up the fire and held her hands out to the flame. When she was warmed up enough she went to the cradle, and followed her course of many nights. The old woman coughed; but no sign was there of the husband. The woman was gone out the door once more before the husband arrived in he kitchen.

He confessed to the old woman that although he saw his wife with their child he was too frightened to approach the apparition.

Next morning, he walked over to the house of his wife's parents. He related to her three brothers what had transpired. The eldest brother shouted that if he had been there he would have held her. In which case, the husband invited him over that night to suit his actions to his words. But since words trip easily from a bragging tongue it was perhaps little surprise that neither the eldest brother nor her husband managed to arrive in the kitchen in time to prevent the mother's departure once more.

A similar path was followed by the second eldest brother who also failed to be on the spot in time, although he promised much in his declarations of valour.

After much discussion between them, it was agreed that all three brothers including the puny youngest brother would lie on the husband's bed that night and keep watch together.

Lying on the outside of the rough bed the youngest could easily be the first to run down to the kitchen to catch his sister.

She came in as she had done previously. This time, though, she kissed the child three times during her preparation for departure instead of the usual single kiss. It was then that the youngest brother leapt up and raced to place his arms about his sister in the kitchen.

Once caught, she screamed and begged her brother to let her go; but he would not do so though it was all he could manage to hold on to her.

In their struggle, she lifted the young man up into the rafters, beseeching him to release her. She cried she would be killed if she was not back in time. But, the youngest brother kept his hold of her though she dragged him about, almost taking his life in the process.

For his part, he shouted to either of his brothers to come to his assistance. One did so and the two brothers struggled with her until she fell down on the floor in a dead faint. The other two men arrived in when the struggle was done and helped restrain her until daylight came.

Next morning, her husband went with one of the brothers for the priest. The priest hurried over to pray over her until ten o'clock in the morning when the day was well set and night was done.

All the while her young brother held her while she returned to the land of the living.

When she recovered her speech, she told the priest that last night was to have been her final visit, as the fairies with whom she stayed were moving to Ulster and she was to go with them.

Now that she had been rescued from the fairies and it was established she had not passed out of this life in childbirth but had been abducted by the fairies, with them leaving a false woman in the bed in her stead, she remained with her husband and child.

To the curious eye, she was much the same as before her disappearance, except that she had a wild look in her eyes until the day she died.

She bore nine sons to her husband after her rescue, and they came to be known in that place as the children of the dead woman.

That is according to an original story related to the story collector Liam Mac Coisdeala by Eamonn a Búrc (62), a tailor from county Galway, who heard the story from his grandfather before that. It is in the Irish Folklore Collection for all to see along with many similar stories of fairy abduction.

8

Beware of handsome men

A brace of stories to do with the machinations of the sidhe collected in the mid-1800s by Jane Wilde mother to Oscar.

Moira

A young girl lived in a different part of the country. Her name was Moira. She had a mortal lover, a fine young fellow, who met his death in an accident.

In the time that followed it seemed that continuing with her life was an impossibility. On an evening not long afterwards, she sat by the roadside at sunset loosing great wet tears of sorrow down her face. She did not notice the beautiful lady dressed all in white; until the lady rubbed her finger to her cheek.

Moira should not cry. Telling the girl that her lover was safe, the lady urged her to take a ring of herbs she held out to her. If she looked through the ring she would see her lost companion, once more, said the lady. Moira was assured that her lover was in good company and was even now waiting for her.

She looked through the ring of herbs. There was her lover in the middle of a great company, . He was pale, but handsomer than ever. He wore a golden circlet on his head and a scarlet sash round his waist. It seemed they had made him a prince.

The lady offered a larger ring of herbs. Whenever Moira wanted to see her lover, she was to pluck a leaf from it and burn it; a great smoke would arise, and Moira would fall into a trance. Her lover would carry Moira away to the fort where he now was. There, she might dance all night with him on the greensward.

She was to say no prayer, nor make a sign of the cross while the smoke was rising, or her lover would disappear forever.

A great change came over Moira from then on. She said no prayer. She cared for no priest, never made the sign of the cross; but every night shut herself up in her room, and burned a leaf of herbs as she had been told; and when the smoke rose she fell into a deep sleep and knew no more.

In the morning, she told how while she seemed to observers to be lying in her bed, she was far away with the fairies on the hill dancing with her lover. She was very happy and wanted neither priest nor prayer nor mass anymore.

Shivers went through her listeners when she said the dead she had known when they were alive were there dancing with the rest; and they welcomed her and gave her wine in little crystal cups, and told her she must soon stay with them and her lover for evermore.

Moira's mother was a good, honest, religious woman, and fretted over her daughter, for she knew the girl had been blasted by the sidhe.

On one night, when Moira went to her bed and was alone in the room, her mother crept up to look through a chink in the old door. She saw Moira take herbs from a secret place in an old brown wooden press. She plucked a leaf and lit it. A great smoke arose and her daughter fell into a trance.

The mother could no longer keep silent. She fell on her knees and prayed aloud for Mary Mother to send the evil spirits away from the child.

She made the sign of the cross over the sleeping girl. Moira started up on the instant and screamed to her mother that the dead had arrived for her.

Her features looked like one in a fit. Her mother sent for the priest, who came at once, and threw holy water on the girl, and said prayers over her. He took the ring of herbs and cursed it for evermore. It became powder in his hands and fell like grey ash onto the floor.

The evil seemed to leave Moira; but for all that she was too weak to move or to speak, or to whisper a prayer.

Before the clock struck twelve that night she lay dead in her mortal bed, despite all the prayers that anyone could say over her.

****

The Rock

Love comes about in different ways. Often the path is stormy and the relationship damaged beyond repair, and lost. Other times, truce follows mayhem and noise. Sometimes, the couple live happily, or, uneasily, together to the end of their days: whether that be love or not is a matter for contemplation. And sometimes the denizens of the Otherworld take a hand; as they did in a troublesome pairing in County Galway, long ago.

There was a man on Shark Island who would cross over to Boffin Island to buy tobacco, but when the weather was too rough for the boat to put out his ill-temper was as bad as the day.

He was married to a decent woman but blamed all ills on his wife, who had no hand act or part in his misfortunes but only tried to keep herself as far away from him as she could.

On those days he would strike his wife, and fling all things inside and without the house about him in a temper to torment and upset her all the more.

On one storm-filled day, a red-haired stranger appeared at the door, without reason or warning, to ask what the husband would give to the man to go to Boffin and return with tobacco for him? But the bully said if the stranger could go, why then so could he, and why should he pay him at all?

In which case, the stranger said he would show him how to travel, but warned that only one could make the journey from the island on this day, while the other would remain on the shore until his return.

They left the house and went to the sea, not far distant away. Arrived by the water's edge, they saw a great company of horsemen and horsewomen galloping along, with music and laughter sounding all about them, while the storm raged high in the sky all about them.

A fine stepping horse was made ready for him, which pleased him, for it seemed to him to be a recognition of his place in life, even though he did not possess as much as a donkey himself. The bully hopped up when he was told to do so. The horse soon lost itself and its rider among the press of excited animals.

In only an instant, it seemed to the bully, who now had no concept of time or place or position such was his excitement, they leaped across the sea and landed safely and all together on Boffin. Once arrived, the exhilarated bully slipt from the horse, in great good humour and ran to buy tobacco and re-mounted in exultation at the power experienced in the rush across the sea.

However, his exaggerated sense of self-worth was cruelly arrested on the return journey, for the horses refused to pass a great rock that stood in the sea between the two islands. The riders urged them on but no horse would pass that rock on that day.

They fell to discussing the problem and decided the best and only way forward was to kill the mortal among them.

It was the only way, the horrified bully heard some of them say, not at all quietly.

They carried the protesting man up to the top of the rock and without hesitation threw him down into the churning white sea. But he rose to the surface as swiftly as he could, for he did not want to expire on this day.

Caught by the spluttering hair, they were going to throw him down a second time, to be sure he departed this mortal life, when the red-haired man appeared to plead for his life. Whatever his standing in the Otherworld the captors released the bully to him. The red-haired man bore him safely to shore on Shark Island, whereupon the assembled horses passed the rock and were soon lost to sight.

The bully was glad to be on his own island once more with only the red-haired man to contend with. But if he thought he could continue in his old ways he was mistaken for before he left them the red-haired man warned that the spirits were watching. If he ever again beat his good wife, or knocked about things at home just to torment her, he would perish upon that rock as sure as fate. This he said in such a strong forthright manner that the bully began to shake, even though his wife was watching him with some interest.

From that time on the bully became as meek as a mouse, for he was afraid, as all bullies are, of a force stronger than he. Whenever he went by the rock in his boat, where he was almost drowned, and where he still feared for his life, he stopped for a moment, and said a little prayer for his wife with a resounding *God Bless Her* offered to the sky in as loud a voice as he could manage.

Whether this kept him from evil, or not, both of them lived together afterwards to a great old age. And whether that equated to love or not is hard to say, other than it is a different view of the existence of two people thrown together in life.

In the telling of this story the red-haired man makes an appearance. He appears in many stories of the fairy world, the Otherworld, as the personage that saves and helps and rescues the unhappy mortal, who is quite helpless under fairy spells.

But who called him in onto the island in this case, or how he came upon the tormented woman is not clear. Suffice to say he did. And changed a pair of lives forever.

9

Fairy wife

When an attractive young woman stood hand on hip before Sean at his doorstep in the Rosses in the west of Donegal it was no hardship to pause in his preparation of a meal for one. He waited for her to speak; but she did not. Through having little opportunity to practice his vocabulary by his solitary fire Sean was a man of few words, though he managed to say: 'Come in,' to the woman, after a while. But, she would not go in, that day.

Off she went leaving Sean wondering whom she might be, for he would know a girl's family by the look of her and the way she carried herself. This woman he knew not at all; but he allowed that he would not mind getting to know her.

She came to the door next day while he was about the same task. He invited her in, this time standing up from the blue wooden chair he sat upon in the sun. She declined with a smile and off she went about her business.

On the third day, he was straining potatoes again when the woman came to his gate. Sean was dressed in his best knitted pullover, massgoing trousers, and his best clean shirt. He had forced his feet into his single pair of boots, a task made more difficult because the boots had the dried-up shape of his dead father's feet in them.

He gestured to the interior of the two-windowed house and invited the woman in. To his delight and surprise she stepped in to Sean's house.

She not only went in but she lived with him as man and wife without the sanction or blessing of priest or minister, or the leave of anyone else.

A year later, she gave birth to a son, to the delight of Sean who was by now planting extra potato beds in the south-facing field for the future needs of his growing family. Not that the child was able yet to sit up and eat a plateful of white fluffy spuds. It was something he thought he should do as a father.

She never said where she came from nor who her family might be; nobody ever called to say they were kin to her nor did she ever express a wish to go and visit cousins or sisters or brothers or parents she might have had before she stepped through Sean's door. He was her chosen husband and mother to their son, for that Sean was grateful.

A while after the boy was born the harvest fair was held in Glenties to the south of their place.

Sean said he thought he might go to the fair. He wanted to meet his friends. Besides, he had uncles living there that he had not seen in a long time, meaning from before the day he had ceased to be a single man living in the family home on his own. His wife said he should of course go.

Sean met his uncles as expected. He was happy to see them for he wanted to say he was a father now, in his own right. But instead of coming to him, it seemed they were avoiding him. He stood in front of one of them and asked: 'What crime do you think I have committed for I have not met you for such a long time, and all you do is shun me before everyone else in the community?'

Angrily, his uncle replied that all agreed they should shun him for he had married a fairy woman.

If Sean had come to them first, they would have selected a good wife for him, and Sean need not have taken up with the fairy woman at all.

'She will have to go, for the good name of the family,' declared his uncle.

That was strong enough but then his uncle shocked Sean altogether. He had brought him a new knife, unused for any other purpose. The knife was for Sean to kill the fairy woman, when Sean returned home.

Without argument and in the face of his uncle's anger a confused Sean took the knife from him and turned for home. He understood his extended family's anxiety. Even so, he had no wish to kill the mother of his child.

Once he was away from the market he threw the knife into a field of corn on the way home. His wife was sitting in the kitchen when he got there as if nothing was astray at all. She asked how he passed the day; to which he replied that the day went very well.

But, when he reported falsely that his uncles were in good form, she replied angrily that Sean should tell her the truth. She told an astonished Sean that one uncle could tell him he had married a fairy woman. And they bought a knife for Sean to take away her life. To which a saddened Sean could only agree and agree again when she asked if he threw it into the field of corn?

In very much quietened tones his wife rose from her seat to say she was going to leave him now. He could go to his uncles, and let them pick a mortal wife for him. She took their child with her, despite his pitiful protestations.

However, every evening Sean was to leave a light burning and some food out for the child and herself who would return to feed in the night.

Though he grieved in every hour of the day, it wasn't long after that when Sean married and brought a new woman into the house and into the bed he had shared with the fairy woman.

His fairy wife and their child came every night into the kitchen to eat. Once, when Sean and the new woman were in bed, she turned her head to see the fairy woman and her child eating their food. The woman in bed gave a cutting laugh that echoed through the house.

The fairy woman said it was a laugh the new woman would cry for. She left the house with the child there and then and never returned.

By then, Sean had prospered in life and wanted for nothing. However, from the next morning, his cattle began to die one by one until there were none. All that remained to him of his livestock was a mare and her foal. Then, it happened that one Tuesday morning early the frightened mare galloped over a cliff, to tumble to the Atlantic rocks below.

Sean put the foal on an island to keep her from harm and when that foal was ready, he took her off the island. Off he went walking along the road to the market to sell her, provided he got the right price.

On the way, Sean came to a place where the cliff face ran close to the road. To his amazement, a door opened in the wall of rock before him, and a boy stepped out who looked familiar but if he was his own son then he had changed a lot since Sean had last seen him, many years ago.

The boy offered five pounds for the foal. Sean said he could get better in the market and walked on. The boy called after him to say that if Sean was offered more than five pounds, he should take it. If not, Sean should return to the door in the cliff above the sea and the boy would give five pounds for the animal.

Though Sean remained at the market with her until the evening, no bid made five pounds. The boy was waiting silently for him on the road on his way home. Without a word between them, Sean gave him the animal's lead. The boy said he should come in and he would pay him.

They went through the door into the cliff. Sean was not at all surprised to find his fairy wife sitting by the fire as if she was at home in their own house. She said to the boy to give Sean five pounds more, and then five more. The boy did as he was told.

His fairy wife said to Sean that he should go home for he had cried enough for the taunt his mortal wife gave on the last night the fairy woman and their son were in that house.

She said Sean should go buy cattle and sheep with the price of the foal. She said the boy was their son. It would not be long until Sean was well off again, she said.

Sean left them and went home and bought new cattle and sheep with the price of the foal, as he was bid. He prospered from that day and was a snug man until the day of his death, though no child nor offspring walked behind his coffin on the day they put him below the ground to join his mortal wife who had given up the ghost long since, though not before she had made Sean's life a misery with her caterwauling about everything that happened in a day, for she was a vexatious person from the moment she came into the world to the day she stepped out of it.

Of the fairy woman and her child no more was ever heard.

10

A touch of an apron

Máire's brother, Peadar loaded their family cart with brimming churns of buttermilk. He roped up Bábín, their little donkey, to pull it along. Máire made her early way to the crossroads with other local girls to begin the day's selling.

Máire passed three sheep, a few cows, and some goats at the front of the house. She heard the younger children crying and laughing and arguing, as she left.

She always got to the marketplace early to secure her place beneath the big chestnut tree. She liked it there for it kept the buttermilk cool on hot summer days when flies buzzed about the churns for what they could steal away from the swishing hands of the fussing sellers.

Most times, there were ten or twelve churns of milk at the crossroads for sale, all with their individual sellers. A great demand existed for the milk, for it was cool and lined the belly well.

Máire combed her long brown hair assiduously and well so each gleaming strand seemed to have a life of its own. Then, she combed it some more, for she did not know if this was to be the day when she would meet someone to fall in love with and who would love her in return, forever.

At the cross a little group of her regular buyers were waiting for her. Some had heir own jugs to take their portion home for the day's use. Others simply had a tin cup bought from a travelling tinsmith for a few coins. They would drink the buttermilk on the spot and go about their business.

Máire stood beside her cart, dressed in her wrap-around apron, and measured out portions to everyone. Most were happy to chat and tell stories they had come across since last they saw one another. With a slim hand she dropped the coins received into her apron pocket,.

A few young men tried to seduce her away from her work and away with them. She laughed and pushed them away; some with words, others with a companionable push and a disapproving look.

All fell away. But some said they would return on the next day to see is she was feeling any looser then. Máire assured them they would fare no better; but if they brought a quart jug with them she would happily sell them delicious buttermilk fresh from the farm.

Sales were busy at first, but as the morning wore on buyers faded away; even those who arrived later than everyone else departed once they had bought some milk. When even the laggards have been attended to, Máire still stood by her little cart. She took a small mouthful from some currant bread that she brought with her to eat until she returned to the farm for a meal of potatoes and bacon and cabbage, all from their own resources. She chewed slowly for the bread was hard and needed to be chewed well by strong teeth.

Brushing a crumb from the side of her mouth, Máire remained by the cart with her serving measure in hand. The churn was not yet empty; but Máire prided herself on not bringing home any milk after a day selling at the cross. She was the champion seller in her family; not even Peadar could come near her.

The crossroads were at the top of the town and from here, she could see the little harbour below.

A wooden ship was tied up at the quay wall while its cargo of boxes and barrels and sacks was unloaded. Local men stood on dry land and caught the swinging loads as they came out of the ship in holding nets. With much argument, oaths and contradictions the cargo was landed safely, eventually.

It was a warm day, and, the work of unloading the cargo before the tide changed called for energetic attention. Máire had been watching from a distance for she knew it to be thirsty work. The workers and sailors sometimes made their way to the cross and to the milk sellers to take some shade and libation when their work was done.

Two of the crew walked up toward the cross now where the milk sellers stood wondering whether they should leave for home, or stay.

One turned to Máire to ask what price her buttermilk was today? He was handsome in a dark way, his skin more sallow than any local boy, his eyes were deep brown, a quiff of hair that fell across his forehead he moved from his eyes in an absentminded way, with a delicate hand that seemed to command hidden strength.

In an unusually dry voice Máire responded to say her buttermilk was a penny a quart. He said he would buy it, but he had nothing with which to drink it from, and what would she suggest?

Máire produced a pint saucepan from beneath the seat of the donkey cart. She did not lend it lightly; for it belonged to her grandmother.

'If you empty it of the first pint I will pour the second one in as soon as you are ready, she offered'.

She tried to keep her voice businesslike though her breathing was most uneven in his presence. He handed Máire a brown penny, lightly touching her fingers in the transaction; not quite by accident. Máire slipped the coin into her apron with the others. Though she knew it to be real, in its falling it had a different timbre to her ear.

The sailor put the saucepan to his parched white lips and drank deeply. Finished, he returned the saucepan. She refilled it as steadily as she could manage without spilling any. Her treacherous fingers would not cease an excited swaying as if they were dancing to a tune she could not hear.

The sailor and his companion waited patiently for the buttermilk to be re-filled. They acknowledged, with a smile, the curious stares of the local maidens for whom they were exotic creatures. The girls gazed at the pair, wondered, and, blushed bright pink.

Meanwhile, Máire flicked her hair backwards to keep it away from her work. Finished his second measure, her customer handed the saucepan to his companion. Máire could never say in the time that followed whether she served the second sailor or whether she left him to fend for himself.

For the man with the deep brown eyes had spilled some drops on his chin when he drained the milk from the saucepan. Máire could only gaze at the glistening drops on his stubbled face. She so much wanted to wipe them away.

Instead, he reached down to dab his mouth with a corner of her apron. And with a farewell he and his companion walked off, leaving Máire bewitched.

They walked very slowly towards the harbour, in no hurry now their work was done. The distance between them and the milk sellers grew further and further.

But, in a move they would talk about for years and years in the town, and to the astonishment of the other milk sellers, Máire quite suddenly jumped from the cart where she had been tidying her effects in a vain effort to calm herself.

She abandoned donkey and cart and churn. Away with her down the street after the stranger. She cascaded along with no heed for anything, as her bare feet sped down the hill. Her eyes were only on her quarry. Then, just as suddenly as she had raced after him she slowed and fell behind for something seemed to hold her back.

She followed on and when the men entered a public house near the harbour Máire followed. She stood silently by the sailor who had touched her apron. There she remained, for no matter what friends or relatives did to separate her from his side, she would not budge.

Word was sent to Peadar to come in all haste while others secured the donkey and cart and churn and what was left of the unsold buttermilk for the family. Peadar came down the street at a trot to veer into the public house where his innocent sister Máire and the two sailors were standing at the counter. His sister had her back to him.

Peadar took his black hafted knife and in one single movement cut the string of his sister's apron. It fell instantly to the floor in a silence that echoed through the watching crowd. For Peadar knew that all who were in the town that day could not separate her from the sailor until the apron was taken off her.

No sooner did the cloth fall to the ground than a bewilded Máire turned and left the company of her own accord.

Without speaking to anyone, she walked carefully back to her cart and its churn at the crossroads and sat up on the board. She turned wordlessly to drive home with Bábín clipping along at a steady trot putting distance between them and the strange goings-on of the day.

For their part, the sailors walked to the water's edge and were never seen in that town again.

While in the public house, Peadar picked up his sister's apron with its severed string to ball it into one firm fist. Taking it into the kitchen, he placed it in the centre of the fire, making sure none of it was left not to be consumed.

The young man stood with careful attention until the cloth burned away completely.

But before Peadar placed the apron on the fire he took the collected coins from its pocket, excepting the brown penny paid for a quart of buttermilk on a hot day at the crossroads.

That penny he left in the dancing flames.

11

Milk of love

When a restless, inquisitive, Cearbhall Ó Dálaigh is told not to take the first milk from an enchanted cow that lives on his grandfather's farm, how can he resist? He does not see drops of milk spilling onto his breast. In his anger, grandfather says Cearbhall will live to regret his disobedience.

Young Cearbhall wonders how drinking milk can cause such a fuss. But grandfather shakes his head, for once the Love Spot, the Ball Seirce, is there, his adult grandson will find anyone exposed to it will follow its bearer anywhere.

By manhood, Cearbhall accepts adoring love often and widely until he meets Aoife the most beautiful woman he has seen in his life. As much as Cearbhall attracts others, Aoife steals the hearts of men like no other. The pair fall for one another. They marry.

They live happily together. An ever-restless Cearbhall is so proud of Aoife that he asks if anyone has ever seen a woman as beautiful, anywhere, as his Aoife?

All agree that it is scarcely possible for there to be a wife as beautiful as Aoife.

For her part, Aoife is pleased she has married Cearbhall. Even still, women try to seduce him with swaying hips and sweet laughter. Aoife makes sure the mark on his chest is covered to all lusting eyes but her own.

In their happy household, food and board is offered freely, for it is a resting place for all who wander past on the way to a distant place.

Nonetheless, to Aoife's increasing frustration, Cearbhall asks each if they have ever seen a woman as fine as his Aoife? Each allows there is none as fair as Aoife. While Cearbhall is delighted with the world's approval; Aoife sometimes wonders why Cearbhall asks the question so often.

On fine May mornings, she bathes in the dew of the hawthorn blossom for it is known that in doing so, skin becomes more beautiful. Aoife keeps a sprig of hawthorn blossom close by for it will increase fertility, people say.

Then.

On an early summer evening a visitor agrees that Aoife is the finest woman he has seen, in this part of the country. Cearbhall asks the man why he says what he says in that way? The man says he meant neither harm nor insult, to either.

The man says he was mistaken; his memory is not what it used to be, what with walking the roads with the dry wind flying and hissing around his face and the soles of his feet calloused with meeting the hard earth, it is a wonder he can remember his own name. He says it was a different woman altogether. Not at all in the same league as the fine woman in whose home he passed the night.

Still, Cearbhall persists in knowing where this woman lives and what her name might be? For the first time he hears the name of *Eibhlín Kavanagh.*

In those two words is a life to change. Aoife recognises what it means in her man and pays him more attention to him than ten men might receive in a lifetime.

Cearbhall's mind will not let him rest for he wonders how there could be someone more beautiful than Aoife.

His journey is long, taking him down many roads and through glens and valleys and over hills and water courses and lakes until it seems that even the landscape that meets his eye every morning is more alluring than any he has left behind.

For all that, his thoughts are confused, for he loves Aoife, yet is drawn to a woman whom he knows only by name.

However, when he arrives at his destination, and sees Eibhlín, daughter of the head of the Kavanagh clan he is lost to all others. Her very movements catch his breath. And, he wonders how he might attract her attention to him.

He hears she has ordered a pair of shoes to be made by a certain cobbler and he contrives to become assistant to the craftsman for he has retained the skills of a cobbler learnt in his youth. His grandfather taught them to him in an attempt to keep the milk of the enchanted cow from his hungry mouth.

The cobbler makes his sample shoe flat, as specified, for Eibhlín is a tall woman. To be noticed for himself, Cearbhall makes his shoe with a small heel. In the event, Eibhlín prefers the one with the heel and asks that the pair be made thus.

The cobbler is busy and tells Cearbhall to make the pair of shoes as he did the sample shoe. In no time at all the shoes are completed and ready for fitting. It falls to Cearbhall to visit Eibhlín's home to test the shoes for comfort.

For a woman who pretends not to notice Cearbhall, Eibhlín contrives to be alone with him for the fitting. With a twinkle in his eye, Cearbhall kneels before her and indicates that she should present her foot to his skilled hand.

Instead, Eibhlín places her foot upon his thigh. He reaches for her and his shirt falls open to reveal the love spot on his chest. While Cearbhall pretends not to notice the effect on Eibhlín's demeanour, he strokes the ankle in his hand to calm its owner so the foot will fit the shoe he has prepared. As the foot finds its snug berth, so too does their love.

But, since Cearbhall is already married to Aoife there is little reason to believe the head of the Kavanagh clan will show anything but righteous anger to the man who has seduced his daughter. He will seek retribution, that much is sure.

To be away, Cearbhall and Eibhlín take her father's best horse and are soon many miles from her parent's household. Using a childhood ruse, Cearbhall reverses the shoes on the horse's hooves so their pursuers will follow the wrong direction.

But if new unfettered love is reckless, then the angry pursuit of a wronged father is relentless. In this case it is successful and the earnest pursuers come on the pair as they rest in one another's arms. They are taken. Eibhlín is escorted home and kept under constant watch. But life is not made easy for the intruder for Cearbhall is charged and tried in court for the kidnapping of a young maiden from the home of her father.

Cearbhall denies all charges, claiming he is a man in love and not an abductor of young women; besides he says he is of good stock in his own right.

He is asked to prove he can support a noblewoman as his only means of support known to the court are that of a cobbler.

In response, Cearbhall declares that as a well educated nobleman he will write with both hands on two sheets of paper on different subjects at the same time. This he does to the wonder of the judge who would dismiss the charges.

Nonetheless, the power of The Kavanagh is so great that Cearbhall is found guilty and banished to the West Indies. On arrival, he is soon pressed into the service of the king as a soldier.

But, if her father thinks physical separation will end their romance he is mistaken; for Eibhlín takes ship after Cearbhall without let or licence from anyone. She disguises herself as a young man by tying her hair under a common cap worn by many travellers. She allows a single lock to fall down as is the custom of serving soldiers. Landed safely in the blinding heat and riotous colour of the West Indies, after a tumultuous sea journey, Eibhlín finds where Cearbhall is billeted.

On that same day on returning to their barracks, heat-weary soldiers hear the sound of a tin whistle coming from the loft. Cearbhall recognises the playing as that of his true love who had learnt the instrument as a tomboy in her father's gardens from a friendly gardener.

He waits while the unruly soldiers welcome the new member to their group, none recognising her true gender. After hours of tomfoolery among the young men Cearbhall finally makes a space where they can be alone and gently removes her cap. He is unsurprised to see masses of brown hair fall about her shoulders, though it ever takes his breath away.

They kiss softly as though never separated for a moment. They discover their love all over again, tumbling finally into exhausted sleep.

They live happily for a time, as man and woman, once Eibhlín's womanhood is acknowledged and wondered at by so many. But the beauty of Eibhlín Kavanagh causes masculine frustration among men living far from their own home.

An acquisitive officer sets his eye on Eibhlín and does so with devastating consequence. She resists him as she resists all others excepting her beloved Cearbhall. But the officer is determined to triumph and will not be denied.

By then and in near-domesticity, Eibhlín sews the shirts of her warrior lover, always ensuring that heavier material covers the place where cloth meets skin above the Ball Seirce. She takes delight in sewing Cearbhall's name on each shirt.

Before one military encounter, the predatory officer asks an unsuspecting Cearbhall for a loan of a shirt on going into battle. He says his own has become torn and tattered from fighting and he cannot appear thus as an officer to whom men look in battle and whom their enemy will watch for any sign of weakness. Cearbhall agrees to give his best shirt to the officer, for Eibhlín will make him a finer one when he returns.

But instead of wearing the fine shirt into action, the officer runs his sword through it to rip it to shreds before dragging it through spilled blood on the battlefield.

Hurrying home before all others, he brings the shirt to Eibhlín to show what has befallen her husband, though he tried to save him, he assures her.

If he thought he might succeed with a shocked widow he is stunned to see that in sudden and overpowering grief, the life of Eibhlín Kavanagh leaves her for she collapses to the floor. lifeless.

The officer flees. Cearbhall sees the ruined shirt on the ground and knows what has happened. He follows on and runs the officer through with a bayonet.

He returns to his beloved, unmoving, Eibhlín and seeing no future in his grief, he carefully places the bayonet on the floor so the point faces upwards. He falls upon the sharp cold steel and he is no more. He falls beside Eibhlín on the dirt floor, so far from home. Then, while life fades away the Ball Seirce fades from his skin as surely as if it had never been there.

12

Forever young

Oisín was never an ordinary person. For Sadbh, (Sive) his huntress mother, was with child by Fionn Mac Cumhaill when abducted by Feardorcha, her spurned magician lover, and turned into a deer by him. She gave birth to Fionn's son in the wild.

Some seven years later, Fionn came upon the wild naked boy deep within a forest. He was named Oisín by Fionn who saw his beloved Sadbh in the boy.

Oisín learned the ways of his father's people and became a warrior of the Fianna but is best remembered as a lover by sweethearts everywhere, and as a poet and storyteller. And for his great love for Niamh of the golden hair.

Niamh and Oisín were first met while Oisín was walking on the seashore with his father. The day was bright and fair. A breeze touched their lips and eyelashes while they walked along in easy companionship speaking of nothing much in particular. The ground before them was freckled with sunlight escaping through the leaves of the trees near the shore. Oisín threw a stone over the water to see how far he could make it skip along the waves.

Fionn first saw movement away to the west, a shimmering apparition dancing upon the water. Neither had seen such a thing before, not in the wilds of the forest nor on the hills or shores of the entire island. A white horse with a floating mane that mirrored the dancing waves approached them with certainty. The wind caught the rider's golden hair and blew it wildly about.

That horse and rider were intent on crossing their path was not in any doubt.

In silence, they waited even as the rider slowed to meet them. Fionn spoke first. He made formal welcome. He asked the rider whom she might be? They could see the visitor had such soft skin it was almost translucent. Her lips were like crushed berries, her pale blue eyes seduced each of them. Without question, and forever.

'I am Niamh na Chinn Óir. I am daughter of Manannán Mac Lir, who rules Tír na nÓg,' she replied in a voice that touched each man with instant longing.

'You are very welcome here. We have heard of the mighty Manannán Mac Lir. His daughter is welcome. I am Fionn Mac Cumhaill, leader of the Fianna that guards Ireland on behalf of our High King. You will accept our hospitality?'

He had not named his son, for he wished to see what this visitor had in mind.

'I thank you for your invitation; but I am on a quest to find a particular person and to take him back with me to Tír na nÓg.'

'Whom do you seek?' asked Oisín quietly.

'I seek Oisín, for I am told he is beyond compare in manly ways; that he is a poet of high renown and the women of Ireland fall down before him so he might choose them.'

'If that is what you have heard, then it must be true,' smiled Oisín.

The horse danced and twirled about under the expert hands of the rider. She checked it to study Oisín.

'Can any man be as wonderful as this?' she asked.

'He is all these things, surely; but he is no more than I am myself,' he responded easily.

'You are Oisín.'

'I am.'

'Then my journey is half over,' Niamh smiled. 'For I have come to find you and bring you to Tír na nÓg with me.'

She described it as the most delightful place of all where trees stooped down with fruit in season and with leaves and with blossom at other times. Honey and wine were there in plenty. Sweet music played on strings. No wasting away ever came to people there for they never saw death nor disease.

'How am I to travel there, if I decide to go with you?'

'We travel together on this steed.'

Oisín considered what was before him. This beautiful woman had come across the waves to him, sight unseen. She rode an extraordinary animal for no ordinary horse could stay above the water as this one did. She was no ordinary woman but the daughter of the king of Tír na nÓg.

She had fallen in love with him by hearsay alone. And he had fallen in love with her on first meeting.

A love-struck Oisín turned to Fionn for blessing, though he was a grown man in his own standing.

Fionn had not stirred throughout, nor did he move now. In the silence, Fionn saw his dear departed Sadbh in the man now before him. He saw her smile through their son and he saw her sweet face give her assent.

Fionn squeezed Oisín's forearm in his hand, though he knew in his heart he would not see his son again, in this world.

Niamh swayed to one side to allow Oisín to join her on this great adventure.

Oisín swung up behind her. His hand lightly caressing her hip as he did so. They turned to the west and made for the fabled land of Tír na nÓg.

Fionn remained by the water even while darkness enveloped him in a cloak of shadows. He waited until the new dawn bathed the land and the sea once more and when he could see no more he turned to tell his people that Oisín was gone on a great adventure, never to return.

For their part, Oisín and Niamh lived happily together in that enchanted place. Their loving union produced a famous warrior son, Oscar, and a daughter, Plór na mBan (The Flower of Women).

But, as much as he was enthralled with his life in the Land of the Young, Oisín's thoughts turned to home in time.

He had written fine lines of poetry about their children and he wanted to share his joy and his song with the Fianna and the people he loved and held dear at home in his own country. Niamh tried to distract him from such thoughts. Many times she succeeded and he put such impulses aside.

Nonetheless, when he said one fine day with determination that he really wished to see Fionn again she agreed to assist him; but he must follow her advice, she warned. That was to take the white horse with him. He was to be guided by the stallion, he was not to dismount from it, and when the horse turned for Tír na nÓg he was not to resist.

Niamh told him that she was in dread that he would never come back to her through the length of his days. Even though he re-assured her that he would return she warned him not to set foot on the ground of his native land, for if he did so he would stay there, forever, as an old crooked man.

She kissed him long and deeply and there never was as much sorrow in a kiss as there was in their last embrace.

Oisín agreed to all that Niamh said.

Came the day, came the steed, that had changed his life before.

Oisín rode away from Niamh and from Tír na nÓg.

If he thought he was away for three years then he was astonished when he came to the home of the High King to find it deserted, his father dead and all the Fianna scattered and gone.

Even the morning had a damp feel; yellow, and red, and brown leaves grew on intruding trees through the fort where once many people had lived. Roads in and about the fort were strewn with dead leaves. Nothing stirred, not even a bird, nor did the sound of lowing livestock reach his listening ears.

He enquired for the Fianna of a small old crooked man who said they had died off three hundred years ago, and who was he and where had he been, and had he a story to tell?

He declared he was Oisín of the Fianna; but the old man waved him away as a braggart for it was well known that Oisín had gone with Niamh to Tír na nÓg, in love and desire.

In despair, Oisín rode around to inspect the places that used to be; but even the very landscape had changed.

In a while, he felt the horse turn for home. But, as it did, he saw a clutch of men attempting to move a large boulder in a field. They seemed so puny to Oisín that he wondered how they survived life at all.

Ever the helpful warrior Oisín rode over to help. He pushed the boulder with one hand from his easy place in the high leather saddle and saw it roll away with a soft thumping sound.

But, if the boulder rolled, then so too did Oisín when he failed to stay upright in the saddle.

Before he quite realised what was happening, he lost balance and tumbled to the ground where his shoulder re-met his old country. The horse he had arrived on departed in a blink of an eye to bring word of the fate of its rider to Tír na nÓg. For if Oisín had been away for 300 years of human time, not the three years of Tír na nÓg time he believed he had lived, he now became a 300-year-old man lying upon the ground.

It was said he never fully recovered from the shock and afterwards wandered the land telling stories of the Fianna and of Tír na nÓg to those who would listen to him. Until, he heard of a man who had travelled across a different stretch of water by boat, a bishop named Patrick from Wales who brought news of a heaven where souls were re-united by a Christian God.

It was a concept that interested Oisín who thought it might take him back to Niamh and his young family.

The Christian Saint Patrick sought Oisín out and asked him for tales of the Fianna. Oisín was glad to have an audience and told his stories well and fully.

It is how we know what happened in Ireland long ago.

13

Timeless love

It is a complicated matter to reconcile the world of gods with the world of man. In the life of gods, mountains move and seas subside and rise with a magnificence that makes man pause; for when the gods are restless, man must be ever watchful.

And when a god-woman from an enchanted isle falls in love with a man from the human world there are those in both places who will resist their union.

One such was Clíodhna the Irish goddess of love. Through the old stories we know she was the most beautiful woman in the world, in her time.

She dwelt in a place that was and a place that was not. An enchanted isle where none ever grew old and where love ruled all who lived there.

Tír Tairngaire, the Land of Promise, otherwise known as Tír na nÓg, the Land of the Young, was a fabled island that lay off the west coast in the wild Atlantic sea that few have ever seen. It was not given to any mortal to travel to that enchanted place, without reason or invitation. It was a happy place without death or ageing, a place filled with beauty.

Clíodhna herself was most beautiful, as befits a god of love and an inhabitant of such a fine place. However, her love of love was to create a tragedy that is recalled to this day. For Clíodhna fell in love with a mortal man and eloped with him to begin a life together.

The man was Ciabhán of the Curling Hair. He was the King of Ulster's son, and the most beautiful of young men, according to those who were there and who observed such matters. It was when he went to Tír Tairngaire, where Clíodhna lived that they fell madly in love.

It was through an invitation delivered at the height of a storm at sea, that threatened to tear his spirit from his body, that the life and destiny of Ciabhán of the Curling Hair was forever entwined with the life and destiny of Clíodhna.

Ciabhán was a member of the Fianna. Each warrior had to be skilled in arms, athletics and the hunt. Ciabhán was everything he was supposed to be as a member of that fabled band. While Mac Cumhaill liked Ciabhán; many of the Fianna grew tired of him, because not one of their women, married or single, did anything but sigh when he passed by. A great many men made their feelings known to their chieftain.

Ciabhán protested, to no avail, that he encouraged none that were unwilling; nevertheless, the whispering against him grew and grew until it had to be faced.

Much as he did not want to do so, Fionn Mac Cumhaill told Ciabhán he would have to send him away, for he was in dread of what the men of the Fianna might do because of the greatness of their envy.

A resigned but dutiful Ciabhán made his long farewells. He broke many hearts in his going both among women who adored him and men that admired him for all he was, and all they might be.

But leave he must. He bade farewell to Fionn and his allies and to Fionn's magnificent hunting dogs; Bran and Sceolán. Ciabhán travelled with the clothes he wore and his weapons of defence and attack. His curling hair he braided so it would not fly about in combat with any other fighter. Its end was contained by the leather belt that held his tunic tight about him.

He travelled long and far, putting as much distance as he could between him and his former comrades, for he was discontented at the reason for his going, but accepted that Fionn had to decide when faced with conflict.

Ciabhán lodged where he could when darkness fell. None refused him stay or sustenance. Many wished he would remain for longer.

For all the welcomes he received and all the good company with which he passed the nights, Ciabhán was restless. He moved on when journey called him once more.

In time, he grew weary of his countrymen and their land; for as soon as he settled somewhere, there were those who said he was too popular for his own good; so, he decided to leave this island altogether and with that thought he headed south as far as he could go to the foot of the island to where he came to the sea in all its openness.

On the shore was a canoe pulled up from the water's edge. Declaring he would leave Ireland forever, for he could get neither shelter nor protection without ill-will being shown him by someone, he cast off.

He was not far away from the land of his birth when he encountered a great storm. His little canoe was tossed from one wave to the next in the same way that he and his friends in the Fianna had tossed a play ball one to the other. Though he was a hardened warrior, he was still a landsman and knew not whether this terrifying storm would subside, or if he would meet the gods of the deep before long.

He believed he was done for, and would never stand on land again, when he saw a rider coming over the waves towards him.

It was an improbable sight; but one that Ciabhán did not challenge, such was his joy at meeting a fellow warrior in time of need.

Arriving beside him, the stranger said he would rescue the young man if he made a pact with him that Ciabhán would give his service to whoever asked him for help, in any time to come.

Of course, Ciabhán said he would of course do so. This, he swore.

With that, the sea subsided and the rider left him there and was soon out of sight, though Ciabhán watched and watched his silhouette until it grew so small that it was not even a fleck on a quietened wave in the distance. Shortly thereafter he found himself landed, safe and well, in Tír Tairngaire where he received a welcome fit for a royal guest.

It was there he met Clíodhna. As simply as that. They met.

Clíodhna, though she was goddess of love, had never given her love to anyone. But she was as taken by Ciabhán as any had ever been. She gave him her love, willingly and completely, and agreed to go away with him.

When lovers meet for the first time, they are newly united. They have loved forever, for their passion knows no bounds. Such is eternal love. It is known by few.

With eyes only for each other, the lovers travelled back to Ireland in the canoe that first brought Ciabhán across the waves. He pulled mightily on the oars, his hair loose about his shoulders tangled and tossed by the sea breeze that blew them towards his birthland.

Such is the way with such voyages that their little vessel of love beached in the very same place that Ciabhán had cast away from who knew how long ago now?

They were hungry, from all that had befallen them, when they reached land. Ciabhán, vaulting onto land as only a man in love could do, said he would hunt a deer, so they could eat.

He asked Clíodhna to remain in the boat, where they had landed, so he could travel faster and return to her more quickly.

He kissed her on her open mouth and smiled at her lovingly while their hands and fingers touched as they parted oh so slowly as he took his temporary leave.

The branches of the forest were thick but he was of the Fianna and knew how to move swiftly through tangled woods in pursuit of game, he was soon out of sight.

At the same time, the warriors of Tír Tairngaire came after the lovers in great determination. It was their mission to return Clíodhna to her own place. Their many boats danced their swift way across the water in unerring pursuit.

When they reached Ireland the hunters spread out across the countryside seeking the lovers who had shunned a Land of Youth and Promise to return to this place where creeping trees and forests grew down to the water's edge.

Searching along the shoreline, one of their number, Luchnu the piper, came upon the canoe where Clíodhna was patiently awaiting the return of Ciabhán. The journey had been tiring for one more used to the slow passage of time in the Land of Eternal Youth.

Clíodhna, though a goddess of love, was tired in her human form. The lapping of the waves against the hide covered boat persuaded her to drowsiness.

Luchnu, seeing that she was already falling asleep, played sweet airs on the pipes until she fell into a deep slumber.

He kept watch for the warrior Ciabhán who would battle for his love when he saw she was being taken from him. But the excited lover was deep in the forest attending to his first kill since his return to this place.

If the deep forest was still, the sea was not. Waves picked up the beat even as soft music sounded across the quiescent body in the little canoe.

While Clíodhna slept and Ciabhán was so far away as to be unable to protect her, one great wave, the ninth, came up from the sea and swept Clíodhna and the canoe away from a desolate Ciabhán, forever.

Some say Clíodhna was returned to the land from which they had fled, others say she remained in the sea offshore, nine waves away.

From time to time, a wave that is known as Tonn Clíodhna, Clíodhna's wave, rolls into the land. It is said to foretell the death of an Irish chieftain.

Perhaps it is also the heartbroken wail of a lover calling to her own true love, so near and yet so very far away.

14

The borrowing of a lake

A young chieftain once wooed the daughter of another chieftain, whose fort lay by Loch Ennel in County Westmeath. The daughter, whose name was Aednat, meaning little fire, was fastidious about her appearance and demanding of all.

When Cian, the young chieftain, came calling, she agreed she would marry him but would not agree to be mistress of his grianán, his fine summer house, unless she could see as beautiful a lake there as that which lay before her father's house at Loch Ennel. It was a demand that perplexed the young man.

While his fort lay in a beautiful glen not far away, it did not include a lake to satisfy his beloved's demand.

In every other way, her suitor's home was admirable. Verdant hillsides were filled with white cottages where happy families lived. A stream meandered along the bottom of the glen that offered drinking water to animals and where women came to wash family clothes on flat rocks by the water's edge and to engage in conversation with their peers.

Even if a dam was created across the glen, it would take a score of years to fill it to lake size, his advisers said. Building of the dam would require a dozen years before that for all materials would have to be hauled along by man, beast, or cart.

By which time, Cian would no longer be a young man. And, by which time Aednat would have wandered off to someone else, having grown weary of waiting for the lake to be completed.

It was a conundrum that taxed the young chieftain and came between him and peace of mind.

He wondered how could he persuade a lake to move. How could he even borrow a lake?

He had heard a great many stories in his father's fort through the long nights of winter when frost reddened the noses of all who travelled to and from that dún. He had heard stories in the yellow-blossomed spring, through hot wilting summers and even through the time of falling autumn leaves. None spoke of relocated lakes.

It happened that Cian's birth mother was dead. His father took a new wife. She was Breena, an enchantress capable of performing magic, for this was in the time of the Tuatha de Danaan.

That her stepson was troubled was clear to his father's new wife. She observed him at length but was careful to keep her distance. Breena did not wish to interfere in his life. Equally, she could not remain unmoved while he tugged handfuls of hair from his head, as he did in his private chambers, trying afterwards to appear completely normal before others, even with hair missing from his scalp.

On this night, Breena sat by the crackling log fire and studied the hot ashes for portents of things to come. Cian sat near her. She saw him take two or three vicious pulls at his long hair, moaning very quietly to himself.

Speaking softly, Breena gently cautioned him to respect his flowing locks for even when this trial was past a chieftain should have his own hair about his shoulders, she said.

Once he began to speak, he told of his love for this young woman who was the only woman he would ever love in this life, or any other life he might visit in time to come. He related Aednat's demand. His stepmother listened patiently and carefully to his description of his almost unattainable love.

Breena re-assured him that if a lake was what was required then she would provide a lake for him to satisfy his intended wife. That she could promise such a thing and that there could be even the remotest possibility that it would materialise is a reflection of the age, and the belief of man. If gods are the rulers, then it stands to reason that when an enchantress says she will provide a lake without the bother of first building a dam and flooding the local stream for a period of three decades, it could very well happen.

To make it happen as expeditiously as possible the stepmother travelled to the sheiling or dwelling of a sister in the art of magic. This place was on the Connacht bank of the Shannon, some miles away to the west of where the old chieftain and Breena his wife dwelt with the lovestruck Cian.

While Breena was away, the young man continued his courtship of the chieftain's daughter who remained sure she would not accept less in marriage than she had already in her father's home.

Meanwhile, his stepmother now sat in a house snugly situated above a lake that had a pleasant appearance though a local wind blew across it whenever it chose. The water changed colour according to the sky it reflected. It was a restless lake, despite its calm surface.

On arrival, the visitor was hospitably entertained by her sister. Breena knew the lake was the right size for the space in the glen beneath her stepson's fort. If she could borrow it, then she could make the young man happy and his chieftain father content, for he spoke of his dead wife overmuch for the liking of his present spouse.

They dined together in harmony, these sisters in the black arts.

The visitor revealed the obsession of her stepson with this young woman who had agreed to marry him but who had demanded a lake be produced below their marital home, a lake that Breena's mortal stepson was incapable of conjuring up.

And so, the visitor asked her wise and considerate sister to loan her lake to the young suitor. The loan would be until the day of the next full moon. At least that was what the Shannon woman believed was asked of her. In this she was mistaken. For she did not hear Breena add, in a low voice, that it would be the next moon's day --- after a full week of eternity had passed --- when the lake would be returned.

In the end, agreement was made that the visitor could borrow the lake until the marriage was consummated and the newly-weds had survived through their excitement and were settled down, for all time.

Breena went alone to the shore and admired this fine wedding present she was about to bestow on her stepson. It was the best of presents and would make him happy indeed.

It is not often that an entire lake is removed from its place. People and animals become confused when this happens, not to mention the shock to surrounding vegetation and water courses when the lake they rely on simply vanishes. Nonetheless, with a great whirling movement Breena whipped her cloak from her shoulders and swept all the water in the lake into her cloak, without spilling one drop, and triumphantly bore it away.

It was early morning when she arrived at the highest point of their home glen. While she contemplated the future and what she was about to do, Breena's cloak heaved and pushed inside the cloth to be free.

In a moment, she would set it loose; but first she had to arrange that a great wind would come along and fell sufficient trees to form a natural barrier and dam the water from escaping straight away. For without hindrance a lake is just so much floating water, gone all too soon.

Afterwards, there were those who said they were awakened by the sound of trees falling in a great storm. Others said it was not falling trees that made them stir; but the noise of ten thousand waterfalls as the lake escaped from the cloak of the enchantress.

No one was lost to the sudden flood. All those living below escaped to the uplands.

They were hospitably sheltered in the dún of their somewhat surprised chieftain, whom Breena had neglected to inform of her intention to create a lake as a wedding present for her stepson. The bride was won, the marriage made and the couple moved into their new home.

The Connacht enchantress waited until the first moon's day had passed, and again, until the second moon's day was gone. She was distressed by the muddy bed of her missing lake. Under the influence of a hot sun a malodorous aroma arose that did not please her olfactory sensibilities at all. And yet, there was no sign of the enriching waters returning.

In time, her patience became exhausted. In anger, she flew to the house of her deceitful sister-enchantress. She was received with a feigned welcome but wasted no time in hospitality.

She had no time for compliments, nor, for gossip. Though the two moons' days had come and gone, instead of a pleasant lake, she could see nothing but rocks, and mud, and decaying fish. She demanded her lake be restored.

But the Leinster woman said her dear sister 's anger had driven away her memory. She recalled she had promised return of the fine piece of water on the moon's day after the first week of eternity and not before.

The rage of the betrayed enchantress knew no bounds, but she was without remedy. And there the matter and the lake lay.

As for Cian and his new wife they lived together for a long, long, time, and were as happy as it was possible to be after such a momentous beginning to their married life.

15

The bride's song

Eileen lived with her father Seosamh on an island in the Atlantic Ocean. Her father fished the waters from a small canoe when the weather was in his favour; and when it was not, he cast nets from shore to gather in anything that might come to him. On land, he hunted for rabbits, or gulls' eggs.

Eileen had helped since she was a child; by now, she knew as well as her father, almost, where a catch was to be made.

Seosamh was different to other fishermen in that he knew ways to charm the water spirits so he could return in safety to land from wild and wilful waters. He could not part the seas; but he could calm wave and storm until he had made safe passage to shore.

He instructed his daughter on how to do this in her own right. Neither allowed anyone else to know they had this ability lest it fade away when they needed it most.

One day, a stranger's boat, of whom neither father nor daughter had any knowledge, was driven towards the shore. A strong ocean wind flecked the wave tops with dancing white horses while they watched. Sand and foam flew along the shore parallel to the ground below their small cabin. Such was the ferocity of the storm they dared not leave the door of their cabin open for a moment longer than necessary, lest the ferocious wind cross the threshold and rip the roof off from inside their dwelling.

Eileen asked if they could save the people below? Seosamh reminded her that their covenant with the spirits only covered them and theirs; though since Eileen was as yet unmarried there was no one else to consider.

They waited and watched and saw there was but one person in the boat though sea spirits and thrashing waves strove to have more souls join them in the depths below.

For a while, it seemed to Eileen the tiny vessel would be carried along to the south of their island. Whoever lay in the boat would be lost; for there was nothing beyond but the everlasting Atlantic Ocean and the edge of the world beyond that.

They had seen people drowned before; it was inevitable when you live by the ocean that people will be lost. It is the way.

Each prayed for the occupant as the boat kept on towards shore though they could see neither sail nor paddle to propel the boat to safety.

Father and daughter knew where the vessel would meet their tiny strand. They went there and stood at the water's edge while the waves rolled in one after another almost as if to say, our task is done. Seosamh first, then Eileen, put a hand to the wooden gunwale of the salt-soaked boat. They positioned the craft so it pointed directly to the whipping white sands.

The ninth wave came in with a mighty rush to lift the boat and its solitary occupant high above all other waves. It dumped the boat above the high water line before it retreated past the soaked father and daughter as they struggled their way to the now unmoving craft.

In it they saw a young man. He appeared to be dead. His stubbled chin indicated he had not slept for many nights. His coat was of green baize, from which the sea had stripped most of the green. He wore top-boots and cloth over-alls wrapped around his upper legs. All soaked through.

Seosamh found it difficult to find a pulse in his wrist. His face was more sombre than Eileen had seen it in a while. The death of a fellow human being always affected him.

The last time they found a dead drowned sailor on this beach below their home her father had not spoken for a month. For now, he said nothing but pushed at the young man's body in an attempt to call him back from the dead.

The old man was about to give up when a watchful Eileen saw movement on the grey cheek of the patient, a twitch. She looked at her father. He moved quickly to save the life of this castaway on their island. He rolled him onto his side and pumped at his body until the sea water that threatened to drown him was retched up. The heaving body drew strength from each racking gasp. The young man and the old man worked together to catch the departing life and draw it back to this world.

Eileen willed them both to succeed and was happy when death passed over until another time and life reasserted itself.

The survivor was quite a handsome man and handsome men were in short supply here on this island. His hair was pure black, his eyes were deep brown, his nose aquiline, his chin firm. What she saw of his body as her father stripped him bare also interested her.

Together, they carried him home on a sled they used for dragging driftwood from the strand to their cottage. Seosamh peeled off his sodden clothes. He wrapped his body in several old blankets. He positioned him before the fire so that radiant heat enveloped his almost-lifeless body. Eileen warmed up the leftover porridge from this morning and used a wooden spoon to feed the survivor. Heat from the fire spread into his being from the outside and heat from the food warmed him from his belly outwards.

In the days and weeks that followed, Eileen nursed and watched over this new man in her life. His name was Philip, he said in a soft voice that revealed some affection for her, his rescuer.

She told her father breathlessly that his name was Philip.

Seosamh said little beyond marvelling that someone should be called Philip.

They heard him tell as he regained his strength that he was sailing alone when the storm almost overpowered him on the surface of the sea. His sail was carried away, as were his oars.

He tried calling for help; but the wind took the words and flung them through the emptiness that suffocated him. He gave himself up to death. He was surprised, therefore, to find that he was not in hell and dead when he opened his eyes. Instead, he had arrived in heaven where an angel took care of him he told Eileen who found herself becoming quite red-faced in response.

With good food and fresh air and plenty of rest and the resurgent virility of a young man in love Philip regained his strength day by day.

In no time at all, and not to the surprise of the old man, the two young people whispered their love, first to each other, then loudly to Seosamh who was now to be father to both, it seemed.

Somewhat to their surprise, Philip said he had a beautiful house and a great deal of land in Ireland ready for them to come live with him with lots of everything that Eileen could desire. There would be silks and fine clothes to wear and wealth to manage, he had servants who would ensure that neither she nor Seosamh would ever again have to cast a net or row a canoe into a storm.

Though Eileen was torn by the excitement of marriage and life anew, she was hesitant to shake off her life with Seosamh on the island.

However, a wise Seosamh put out to sea for several nights while his daughter discussed their life with her soon-to-be husband.

On his return and hearing of Eileen's commitment to a new life in a different house, Seosamh gave them his happy blessing. They were betrothed. The wedding day was fixed. They would marry on the mainland; but first Philip would bring his friends to the island to show them the place of his deliverance. This, he declared with some enthusiasm.

With all her old certainty, Eileen knew as soon as he spoke that he was in danger. For she knew that a storm would come and test him once more. This time, the boat would be filled with his friends. Such was the way of young men at a wedding party. They know no fear. They allow no challenge they cannot meet.

Eileen knew in her soul that their boat would make heavy going of the passage to the island.

With tear stained face she asked Philip not to leave; or at least to take her with him, to steer the boat. That was all she offered: to steer the boat.

When the foreseen danger manifested itself, she would have power over the waves and the wind and could intercede for his life with the spirits, and the storm.

She dared not tell this family secret to Philip. If she did, it would fail. The charm would be useless for ever after.

But being young and in love and invincible, Philip laughed at her fears. The day was bright and clear so what could happen?

He put off from the strand and reached the mainland in time in safety and without mishap of any kind. As Eileen foresaw, he filled the boat with many raucous males to return to the island.

With trepidation, she saw the laden boat plough towards the island over grey waves.

As she feared, a sudden gust of wind drove the overladen boat onto harsh rocks when they were within sight of Eileen's home.

She could see Philip in the midst of it all looking towards the land in vain for relief. Though the distance was too far for rescue, their eyes sought one another across the water.

The storm upset the boat and all in it perished. Including the groom, once saved, once lost, this time with the flower of his friends by his side.

Eileen heard the surprised, defiant, cries of drowning men; but could give no help. She knew her true love had journeyed to the bottom of the sea with his struggling companions, and would never return to her, alive.

Standing there above the water that had stolen her life from her Eileen sang a death dirge for him, in Irish, the language of her people and which came to her lips from ancestral memory. The sound rose and rose until it seemed to take a life of its own. It quietened the storm and calmed the waves as all listened to her grief.

When the last echoing notes faded into the distance and all was still, Eileen lay down and gave up her own ghost, in silence. She had gone in search of Philip in another world.

Seosamh disappeared from the island soon afterwards to join his own ancestors in the spirit world.

From that day to this no one has ever ventured to live on the island. It is haunted by the spirit of Eileen. Her mournful wailing is heard in the nights when the winds are strong and the waves beat upon the rocks below the house where she lived and loved and died of love.

Of Philip and his companions there has been no sighting ever since their boat was wrecked upon the rocks.

All we have of what was is the sound of the bride's song that comes in off the sea.

16

The lady of Gollerus

On the shore of Smerwick harbour in county Kerry early on a fine summer's morning Dick Fitzgerald stood smoking his pipe.

He was an unmarried man and given to speaking out loud so as to hear the sound of a human voice. His utterances this morning was on his single state. He directed his observations at a standing rock upon the strand. While it could not speak, it stood up as firm and as bold as any living Kerry person might do. On he went allowing everything that was bothering him to spill out of his head the better to clear it.

For all his fine words, early morning light shining through rising sea mist can play tricks with the imagination. Dick Fitzgerald thought he was mistaken when he saw at the foot of the same rock, a beautiful young creature combing her sea-green hair.

He guessed at once that she was a Merrow, a sea woman, although he had never seen one before. He had heard plenty of stories about them for such stories are to be found in many sea-facing nations. On her head she should have been wearing a cochallin draíochta a little enchanted cap, which the sea people use for diving down into the ocean. Instead, it was beside her on the strand, the better to comb her hair, he supposed. Without that cap, she would lose the power of diving beneath the water he quickly realised. Without further thought, Dick Fitzgerald ran forward to seize the cap and hold it aloft in triumph.

If he was happy then the owner of the cap was not. Salt tears came trickling down her cheeks when the Merrow saw what had happened. A low mournful cry came from her that sounded like the cry of a new-born infant.

Though he did not offer to restore the cap to its wretched owner, Dick sat down by her side to take her hand by way of comforting her. He saw that there was a small web between her fingers, and that her hand was as thin and as white as the skin is between an egg and its shell. He asked her various questions to see if she understood him. Getting no answer to his questions he squeezed her hand as gently as he could without causing her any harm. It seemed to calm the tormented one down for she stopped crying at that, according to Thomas Crofton Croker who first collected this story not too long after it happened.

But if Dick Fitzgerald thought she was grateful to him he was surprised to hear her first utterance in a language he could understand.

She asked him with sorrowful eyes 'Man, will you eat me? What will you do with me, if you won't eat me?'

Of course now that he looked at her with a little more inspection Dick thought he would make her his wife and not a meal at all. And when he discovered she could also speak his language he fell completely in love with her.

He told her so and she agreed that she would be his wife if he would just wait until she twisted up her hair. It was some time before she had settled it entirely to her liking. When that was done, the Merrow whispered some words to the water that came close to the foot of the rock.

Dick saw the murmur of the words upon the top of the sea going out towards the wide ocean, just like a breath of wind rippling along, and asked her about it. But his new love assured him it was nothing at all other than she was sending word to her father, the king of the waves, not to wait breakfast for her.

With that news Dick asked if her father had all the money that lies in the bottom of the sea in his keeping?

But his new love only asked him what money might be?

Not bothering to explain the nicety of money, Dick enquired if the fishes had enough understanding to bring up whatever she bade them bring up?

On hearing her certainty that they would do whatever she told them Dick quickly explained that all he had was a straw bed for her in his home. That was no ways fitting for a king's daughter who surely deserved a nice feather bed, with a pair of new blankets to lie on. But confusion continued between them. Further conversation yielded the information that she had fourteen oyster beds of her own beneath the waves.

Dick Fitzgerald was now more determined to marry the Merrow than he had been when he first saw her combing her hair. And she had given her consent to marriage. Away they went, across the strand from Gollerrus to where Father Fitzgibbon happened to be that morning.

The priest was used to strange requests but marriage between a Christian and a fish was too much for him. His advice to the groom-to-be was to send the scaly creature home to her own people.

But a persistent Dick pointed out that she was a king's daughter. The priest replied that she was still a fish and stamped his right foot in its nice black shoe on the hard clay to emphasise his point of theology.

Dick then explained that she had all the gold that's down in the sea for the asking, and it would be his as soon as he married her.

Which changed the priest's perspective entirely. Of course, Dick should marry her by all means if she was ten times a fish; for money was not to be refused in hard times.

To do so would be a sinful waste he pontificated.

The clergyman added that he himself might as well have the hansel of it as another for all the counselling he had rendered to the good Dick Fitzgerald and his intended wife.

Father Fitzgibbon married Dick Fitzgerald to the Merrow, and like any loving couple, they returned to Gollerus well pleased with each other. They prospered and lived together in the greatest contentment and wanted for nothing. At the end of three years, they had produced a girl and two boys as their little family.

However, Dick had not wit enough to secure the tenure of the Merrow.

One day, he was obliged to go to Tralee which was a good distance away. He left his wife minding the children and the household at home while he was away. He thought she had plenty to do without disturbing his fishing tackle. This he always looked after himself being sensitive to his wife's origins and feelings.

He was no sooner on the road than his wife set about cleaning up the house. She did so with such thoroughness that she disturbed a hanging fishing net that was rarely touched. She discovered that the net concealed a hole in the wall wherein lay her cochallin draíochta.

Having given up on ever finding it again she ever so gently drew it out to study it. She thought of her father the king, and her mother the queen, and her brothers and sisters, and she felt a longing to go back to them.

She sat on a little stool and thought of the happy days she had spent under the sea. Then, she looked at her children, and thought of the love and affection of poor Dick, and how it would break his heart to lose her.

But, she reasoned he would not lose her entirely, for she would come back to him again, and who could blame her for going to see her father and mother after being so long away from them?

She went towards the door, but came back to look at the infant sleeping in the cradle. She kissed it gently. A trembling tear fell on the child's rosy cheek.

Softly, she wiped away the tear, and turning to Kathelin the eldest child, told her to take good care of her brothers, and to be good herself, until she came back.

She went to the strand, to the glittering sea that was lying calm and smooth in the sun. When she heard a faint sweet singing, inviting her to come down beneath the waves, all her old ideas and feelings came flooding into her mind. Her land family was instantly forgotten. Placing the cochallin draíochta on her head, she plunged into the sea.

Dick came home in the evening, and missing his wife, he asked little Kathelin what had become of her mother, but she could not tell him. He enquired of the neighbours, and he learned she was seen going towards the strand with a strange looking cocked hat in her hand. He returned to his cabin to search for the cochallin draíochta and soon discovered it was gone.

Year after year Dick Fitzgerald waited, expecting the return of his wife, but he never saw her again. He never married again, always thinking the Merrow would return to him.

Nothing could ever persuade him but that her father the king kept her below by force, for she surely would not give up her husband and her children of herself.

While she was with him, she was so good a wife in every respect that to this day she is spoken of in the tradition of the county as the Lady of Gollerus.

17

Last ride of the lovers

Though the night was dark Máire waited patiently for Cathal by the corner of her father's house. She lived in this house all her life and knew every moaning whistling sound made by the wind through the trees as much as she knew the crackling of the big old whitethorn tree that grew close by the whitewashed house.

She knew the twists of the grass-green drive that sloped to meet the passing road below. She knew how many paces it took to be hidden from view from anyone peering out of the window to see how the night was faring.

Until now, Máire knew this place as her only home. But, tonight she was to embark on her greatest adventure.

Her long hair slipped over her shoulder when she inclined her head to check if she heard a horse's hoof strike a stone in the silent darkness. If she had, it did not repeat.

She strained to be sure the latch had not been raised on the kitchen door, for someone might have stepped out to join her in the silent darkness.

Cathal had promised he would come to her this night and at this time. They would ride away on his horse and live together forever, as man and wife.

They agreed to this course of action , a month ago, when her father forbade her to see Cathal after finding them deep in whispering conversation at the gate.

When Máire demanded a reason, her father would not answer. Máire was the loveliest daughter any man could have, he eventually said. She deserved better than the sweet talking Cathal who had neither land nor money to support a wife and family.

So, they decided that they would run away and be married somewhere they were not known, by a quiescent priest. And if permission was denied by the churchman, they would lie to anyone they met that their union was blessed by a priest on his keeping out on the hill.

For they would bless their own union, vowed Cathal, as he left to go his late uncle's farm to claim the inheritance of a horse that would carry them away to a new life together.

In the time that followed, Máire heard of an accident, in the next county, where a horse bolted and threw its rider, a young man, who struck his head so surely that he died. She hoped that Cathal would not allow that to happen to him.

Still, she waited on in the moonlight. She recalled again how he smiled at her at the dance less than half a year ago and how she knew they were to be together, forever, from that moment.

They had eyes for no other. It mattered not to Máire that Cathal had no land nor guaranteed source of income. Her father was rich and Máire had never known need; so she believed that love would provide.

She saw in her mind's eye the deep incisions of their names in a beech tree near where they first kissed in the soft moonlight.

Perhaps, Cathal would steer the horse that way as they left for their life together. How nice to re-visit the glade where his lips first brushed hers.

She walked to the gate to await him there. Enough time had been wasted in standing still. She just wanted to be with Cathal.

Máire was almost at the gate when she saw the bulk of a horse and rider arriving at the gate. She tried to hold her smile in check. But if ever there was a time to smile it was then, though if Cathal smiled at her she could not see it in the darkness.

Her lover said nothing while leaning down to take her precious bundle of clothes from her. Her clothes were tied up in a colourful shawl that was left to her by her long-dead mother. Once the clothes were secured, Cathal held her by the hand as she travelled aloft to join him on the broad back of the dark horse.

Máire snaked her hands around his hips and squeezed him tightly to show she was so glad to see him that her heart was almost bursting. Cathal shifted to fit more comfortably into her hold. She was content.

All she saw was their life together, Cathal and Máire, Máire and Cathal. While she dreamed away, he turned the horse deeper into the darkness that enveloped them.

Máire did not know where they were going, for they never discussed that at all. She knew it was away from here. And with Cathal.

They rode on. Cathal said little. Máire was content to be with him. There would be all the time in the world to tell one another what they felt about everything, and each other. And the other would sit and listen patiently and nod. This she knew, for she had rehearsed it many times in her mind since she and Cathal first met.

Máire knew they should be at their destination before light spread over the land for a new day. and they could be seen by others or her father would be alerted to their whereabouts.

Somewhere in the distance she heard a cock crow out the dawning of a day; but Cathal said she was mistaken.

His posture seemed to change at that, for there was no cosiness to his shape in her arms any longer. He rode on with more intent. He leaned forward, searching for something ahead.

Máire thought that perhaps he was tired at their flight from all that was familiar. What else could it be, she wondered?

She called out to him to give spur, with his foot, so they might meet their destiny sooner.

He said he had no spur to give to any horse for he had no more strength in his foot than the froth on the surface of the river they were passing by.

These were not the words of the Cathal she loved. They were utterances of a stranger.

While her unease grew, Cathal turned the horse into a laneway she had never seen before.

She realised they had come to a graveyard. It seemed familiar, yet Máire knew she has never been here. Still, most cemeteries have similar appearance in darkness. There are a few sheltering trees, some old headstones lean sideways or forward, depending on their proclivity and the ground into which they are sunk. She saw that some newer markers stood upright refusing, for now, to acknowledge that the corpse they guarded was past caring.

There were some fresh graves, some newly covered in, some newly opened. One such seemed to be their destination.

Cathal swung down from the horse. He held his hand to Máire to help her to join him on the ground. He gave her the bundle of clothes he had kept safe for her. She wondered why he was doing this.

Why are we here? she asked.

In mute reply, Cathal reached out for her with his own arms outstretched.

The cock crew in the distance, this time for sure, of that there was no doubt. Cathal grabbed at Máire with more urgency now.

As is well known, at cockcrow all supernatural beings retire to the Otherworld where they pass the hours of daylight, until darkness returns and they are free to roam.

Confused and unbelieving by turn, Máire stepped back from Cathal's reach. She stumbled. She felt him tugging at the shawl that surrounded her few belongings. They fell from her hands. She wondered if she was dreaming for if she was this was a nightmare.

The grasping fingers of the man before her continued to pull at her clothing despite her continuing resistance.

He roughly said it was a fine night to be out in a graveyard with a striapach like her, a striapach being a coarse word for a woman of easy virtue.

Growing more alarmed, Máire pulled away from him and soon found herself facing away from this man who it seemed was now intent on her defilement in this place of the dead.

She ran away from him as fast as she could; her feet did not even touch the ground that she was aware of. If Cathal was pursuing her she could not hear any footsteps behind her. She ran and ran into the brightening air. As daylight grew stronger, all sound of pursuit faded once she left the graveyard further and further behind.

Sobbing for all she had lost, Máire hurried on.

At her father's home the household was stirring for the day and the breakfast porridge was being poured for all when she arrived in the yard. Máire tried to go to her room unnoticed; but her father reached out to stop her and to enquire where she had been and what was the matter?

Such was her torment that words tumbled from her before she had time to compose a narrative that would excuse the behaviour of her heart's delight.

Her father listened in dread to her tale. He held her so close she almost fainted for want of air. She pushed him away to arm's length. What do you know? she asked with her terrified eyes.

'Cathal was killed a few days ago,' her sorrowful father told her. 'The horse bolted when a bird flew up and he was thrown.'

Whoever she rode with tonight was not the living Cathal, he said more gravelly than she had ever heard him speak.

Máire heard no more for the floor of their house came towards her with great suddenness as she fainted away.

Days passed before she recovered enough to accompany her father to the graveyard where the remains of the recently deceased Cathal were laid.

With dreadful certainty she saw it was the same graveyard from whence she had fled. There they surveyed a newly-dug grave, with no name above it, no marker at all graced it.

However, Máire's bundle was scattered everywhere. Her lost clothes were in torn shreds on the ground.

A visibly shaken Máire saw her best shawl was lying on top of the grave. Reaching for it, she saw she could not lift it up, for damp cloying clay was soaked through it.

With all his strength her father pulled at it but even he could not dislodge it. There it would have remained only that he found a sharp stick on the ground with which to dig deeper. He soon rescued most of the shawl and while he was at it uncovered the coffin wherein lay the decaying remains of the departed Cathal.

Máire saw that the held end of her shawl was inside the coffin of her dead love, her heart's desire, and she fell upon the grave, not quite dead herself but in a heartbroken faint while her father waited patiently to take her home to safety.

18

Tree of the seven thorns

Who can say what attracts one person to another even when they are very far apart in life? None were more apart than the son of a powerful chieftain, and, a barefoot girl in fifteenth century Ireland. A plague and a famine in 1439 ravaged the population, yet love grew in the midst of it all.

The O'Kellys were a powerful Irish family who resided in a fort on a hill. Ulick was the youngest and his father's favourite. His father indulged the youngster in his activities without censure.

Ulick believed local women were his to sport with, as fancy moved him. He found many, married or single, to be willing partners of his fleeting interest.

Nonetheless, for a single woman in the 15th century to become pregnant by a man she was not to marry before the birth of their child was certain ruin, for few men would consent to raising another's as his own. There were no social safeguards for the protection of child or mother, other than the embrace of the mother's birth family. Many families chose to shunt their errant daughter off to wherever they could find a home for her away from the family's reputation for propriety.

Ulick O'Kelly cared nothing for any of this, for the consequences of his behaviour would not affect his position in his family nor his inheritance. In that he was secure.

Despite, or perhaps because of his reputation for abandonment, O'Kelly attracted young women without count. Among these was the beautiful and graceful Oonah More who came from a large but poor family that lived in the smallest of houses at the end of the local village. Oonah too was the youngest in her family of all brothers.

In her curiosity she found herself lingering at the entrance to the O'Kelly lands in the high heat and dust of August. Perhaps it was the danger that made her stay; perhaps it was to catch a glimpse of this man who turned so many heads and stole so many hearts.

Though, true to arrogant form, he passed by on a fine stallion without a glance at her. Perhaps he did not see her; but it was more likely that he did. The result of such disregard was to make Oonah more determined that he should stop to speak to her. Once, when she stood on the road with a spilt basket of fish she was transporting to the market he rode around her rather than offer comment on her mishap. Next time, she managed to spill her wares so close to the horse that it shied away causing its rider to pay attention to the person causing such aggravation. That time, Oonah turned her head away. And on it went so he would have had to have been blind not to notice her.

That he did so after many contrived encounters was not so much an acknowledgement of her attraction as his inclination to add another notch to his belt. He spoke to her with honied words and smooth tone so that an entranced Oonah went with him wherever he led. He brought danger and excitement to her uneventful life. His existence consumed her every thought through autumn days and long nights. He was all she drew breath for.

She loved him with all of her innocence. He welcomed the blank page she offered him. They met in many places at many times and made love often and with abandon.

And when he was finished and his attention wandered to new challenge he abandoned Oonah, by now with child, though she was not aware of it. She attributed her early morning physical discomfort to many causes, until there was no other cause left but pregnancy.

She chose not to tell her lover that she was with child, lest he feel a duty of marriage to her for she still believed he would marry her for love.

She hid her development from her family and from the priests of the parish, and from everyone else though for most there were more pressing matters of survival to be concerned about. Many expired for lack of food, for want of care. Many weakened by famine were unable to withstand the plague and were taken into a death that may have been a relief for some.

Into these days Oonah brought her baby, never revealing the identity of the infant girl's father. Though her sinful behaviour was read out from the altar by disapproving clerics, few people cared about a new mouth to feed.

Her family took the child in as one of their own. In time, wagging tongues quietened to the occasional barb when opportunity presented itself.

Believing the cant of the clergy that she was a sinner; and in personal penance, Oonah gave herself to the care of the sick, risking her own health to bring comfort to neighbours stricken by the plague.

Her older brothers, reasoning correctly who the father of her child was for sure had taken it as a family honour to punish O'Kelly for the torment and shame he had visited upon their beloved sister.

They were on the point of seizing him and putting him to death one dark night when they heard Providence had taken a hand in the dance of life.

Plague is no respecter of position. It attacks the high and the mighty just the same as it visits a humble home. In this horrifying time, graves welcomed a corpse attired in fine clothes as easily as lifeless bodies wrapped in the poorest of rags.

Pestilence came to Ulick O'Kelly, that mighty lover and ruiner of families, in spite of his handsome good looks, his many conquests, and the power of his family.

He was going about his daily life with a quip and a whistled tune one day, and on the next day he was in his bed under the care of the best doctors his father's wealth could persuade to enter the room.

They fussed about the chamber and the house. They stayed as far away from the patient as possible which while if not curing the patient ensured that as much noise and commotion and hand wringing as possible was made at his passing.

The condition of the victim worsened in spite of it all and since he now had the capacity to infect every soul in the place with the plague it was decreed by the doctors and reluctantly agreed to by his father that he should be removed from the company of men. And since he was unable to walk or make his own way anywhere he was transported in a wooden cradle to the side of a field.

A shelter was fixed to keep rain from drenching him and the sun from scalding him. A pitcher of water and a griddle cake, marked with a cross, were left by his side. That both water and cake came from his father's house was of little comfort to the dying man for instead of people being attracted to him, they were repulsed by his condition. They avoided the shelter where he lay even though all could hear his pitiful cries for attention.

Many came to hear his torment and his ramblings, recalling similar desperation and suffering he had visited on them and theirs at the height of his powers.

Some even came close enough so he could hear their mockery of him in his lowly state. Wisely, they kept a distance away so he could not infect them with pestilence as his dying farewell. Some even threw stones onto the roof of his shelter so he might know little comfort or rest.

Other than for his father and his brothers, and not all of them either, Ulick O'Kelly approached the end of his life's journey in a solitary state.

A sorrowful Oonah was moved by the news of his pitiful state. The information was relayed by her brothers, though they would have had preferred to administer justice directly to O'Kelly. Long and excruciating justice, they said.

Oonah reminded them that they claimed he was father to her child. For that alone he deserved some acknowledgement and kindness no matter what the circumstances of her conception.

Without asking for agreement or permission from anyone she made her quiet way to his side under the shaking and rattling shelter far out in the fields among the long grasses. Not really wishing to see her once powerful lover shrunken to near-death, Oonah approached his resting place slowly. The shrivelled form was glad of human company that did not threaten, though she thought he did not quite know who she was.

Oonah offered every little convenience that might alleviate his sufferings, for which he gave her heartful thanks.

So well did she administer to him that from her first visit onwards neither groan nor cry escaped his lips but those that were unwillingly wrung from him by the relentless depredation of his condition.

For days and days, Oonah attended him as his condition slipped lower and lower. She spoke softly to him and awakened his soul to a sense of past guilt, and the necessity of true contrition, even if no priest would come any closer than those who administered the last rites before he was so roughly removed from his father's household.

Over time, his cries faded to whisper. Oonah dutifully refilled the water by his side and collected fresh bread each day at the gate of the field where it was left by servants of his father.

Until, she was observed by those passing along the road to be sitting stock still facing the shelter though no human sound came from there.

Scaldcrows tried to enter the lean-to for food, but were continually driven away by a milk-white bird that perched itself on top of the rickety edifice.

Though more days went by the silence continued. Oonah's figure could be seen in the same position. Unmoving. When carrion birds attempted to enter the shelter, the white bird relentlessly drove them away.

Family called to her across the field to come home. Her work was done. But they knew even as they called out that Oonah's own soul had gone to its home in heaven. Only her ever-attentive body remained they discovered when they ventured closer to appraise the situation.

Accepting the will of God and the determination of the barefooted girl, her family and friends and neighbours placed Oonah's body beside that of the decayed sinner and ravager of hope and future.

They set fire to the shelter, bodies, and all, in a funeral pyre that rose to the heavens and spread its ashes and reeking odour over all so that people placed old clothes about their doors and windows to keep the smell of rotting corpse away.

Nonetheless, from those same ashes in time sprung a tree that was to become known as the Tree of the Seven Thorns.

On its branches a white bird emits melancholy notes, never stirring from its perch at the approach of man or woman.

For good or bad.

19

Mother's love

The love of a mother for her child will survive beyond the last breath.

Bride Liath Ni Shúilleabhain lived by the sea in Coumeenole on the Dingle peninsula, in the mid-1800s. Her surname in English was O'Sullivan. At the time, women kept their birth family name on marriage. Bride was a sought-after spinner of wool. She travelled throughout the parish of Dunquin and to the offshore Blasket islands earning money to help raise her family of eight children.

Their small house was 20ft in length and 13ft wide for ten people to live in. It stood on the outskirts of a number of similar houses. In the house was a kitchen and a bedroom. They lived in the kitchen and slept in the bedroom. A fishing net was folded up at night to make a bed on a bench by the turf fire. Wherever there was room to lie down, thin mattresses were stuffed with seabirds' feathers and laid out for sleep. Fine sand was shaken on the flattened clay floor to keep it clean and dry in the face of many young feet trampling all over it in a day.

In their growing years, Bride and her husband taught the children how to clean their neat home, fish, cut turf, sow potatoes, and other practical matters they needed to know. Bride showed her daughters how to spin wool. In the evenings, they went to hear music and storytelling in neighbours' houses. They said their prayers, and learned respect for others.

Happy as they were and used to challenges that confronted their lives, they were unprepared for a sudden and devastating famine, no more than their neighbours.

The core potato crop failed throughout the country, in the mid 1840s, attacked by a blight, unseen until then.

Through Bride's spinning work, the family had other means of staying alive when the potatoes rotted in the small garden beside the house. However, their neighbours, and Bride's buyers of her spinning skills, had no money to pay her, nor, any interest in purchasing anything not edible in a time of famine.

While food grew scarcer in the years of suffocating want, Bride's husband quietly went without food so his children could eat. Nonetheless, an empty sack cannot stand for long. He weakened and passed away as quietly as he had lived. His family wept and mourned for him.

His death increased the crisis for the family for he had been a good provider of food even if that amount was small compared to its need. Hunger spread deeper into the small household, taking away the youngest and the oldest.

Bride could only weep as she watched her loved ones go from her, one at a time, while she could do no more than draw a shroud around their famished forms. It was not for this task that a mother gives life.

Death took each of them from Bride's weakening fingers until she was left with only one, the middle child, a girl they said afterwards had the finest and most beautiful presence seen in Kerry for years, when she was in her full health.

But beauty cannot deny death nor delay it when it calls. Bride fought with all her will to deny death this final prize of her lovely daughter; a child haunted by the memory of her own dying siblings.

Bride had been grateful that God had left her one daughter even though two people lived where ten had jostled shoulder-to-shoulder in the small house that now seemed so cavernous.

However, the Fates were not yet finished with Bride. For in the wake of the famine that had taken so many lives came a cholera epidemic to swathe through those still standing. It took away the last child of Bride O'Sullivan.

Bride closed her daughter's eyes so she would never again see want or torment. And she sat for a while, wondering what to do now that her remaining child was gone. Since people were terrified, and remained indoors, hoping the plague would not reach them, there was no one to help Bride bring the corpse of her daughter to the graveyard, dig the grave and bury her in God's earth, saying prayers for the repose of her soul. Even if there were, Bride had no money to pay for a coffin.

But to a consecrated burial ground she must take her last child so she might be with the others on the day of the Resurrection when all bodies would be re-united with their soul, according to Bride's religious belief.

Bride was accustomed to working with her hands and so she fashioned a long carrying harness out of straw rope known as sugán twine. This twine had softened the seat of the few chairs they sat upon when the house rang with laughter and argument and trickery of all sorts.

Into the harness Bride placed her dead daughter and hoisted her onto her thin back. But, if she was weak herself there was no weight at all in the few bones of her deceased child.

Before stepping from interior gloom into daylight, Bride blessed herself and her daughter from the tiny holy water font hanging from an old nail driven into the wooden door frame. The traditional blessing was to keep the wanderer safe until they returned to the safety of home.

Though it was of little use now, Bride completed the ritual, hoping it might count in the scales of heaven for her family's sake.

For despite all that happened Bride still had trust in a merciful God.

She began the journey, shuffling along, resting, stumbling sometimes, all the while drawing closer to the cemetery.

But it was not a straightforward journey. Bride had to cross a stream on stepping stones at the bottom of the hill and climb up again towards Dunquin graveyard. She proceeded carefully and patiently for she did not want to roll down the grass and into the water with her dead daughter strapped to her back.

Though the journey was strewn with obstacles and challenges, and took a long time, Bride arrived safely inside the graveyard and lowered her burden to the ground. However, she was so spent that she had not the strength to open the grave with her bare hands even though the grass had not had a chance to re-grow roots since the last interment of one of her children.

Somehow in the midst of her torment, it seemed to Bride that some local men were sent by God to help her, for they were passing and saw her desolation. After some hesitation, they opened the grave for her with the ease of strong men used to this work. They waited while Bride moved the body of her dead daughter into place in the shallow declivity. They filled in the grave and departed with a mumbled prayer.

Bride remained alone to sing a soft lament. It was a song she often sang in the evenings to calm the older children and to soothe the younger ones to sleep.

When it was done she remained sitting in silent contemplation before she whispered softly to her loved ones that they should sleep in peace, now, for no sod of grass would ever be lifted from their grave.

So saying, she left the graveyard, never to return in this life.

Bride started on the painful road home to Coumeenole, the empty sugán harness in her lonely hands. There was nothing left for her to be bothered about. In time, death would come for her and she would end her journey with resignation, this she had decided at the grave side.

On her way along she was hailed by a caring neighbour: Nora de Londra, who waited for her near the stream she had lately crossed with her burden. Nora invited Bride into her home and sat her by the turf fire. She gave her food and sat with her. Nora offered Bride lodging for the night if she needed or wanted it. She would be very welcome in this house she added.

Nonetheless, Bride gave her thanks for the food and the impulse, and took her leave in due course and with all civility.

But, if she thought her travails were over she was mistaken, for when she came to the home she shared with her family of eight and her fine husband she was to see that the people of the parish had burned her house to the ground. It was the only way to ensure the cholera inside the house would be banished from their midst. they said

All that stood now were four walls with a deep heat crack down the gable end where the chimney was.

That Bride had no house and no family to cheer her days was not something anyone would talk about. She understood why it was done. But the doing of it meant that all she possessed, all she called her own, little enough that it was, was now as if it never was at all.

All she had were the clothes she stood up in to call her own. Still in her hand was the sugán rope she had carried her last child with to the graveyard. Bride had no reason to remain in Coumeenole, now, where the smell of burning and pestilence hung in the air wherever she turned.

With not a single backward glance, she walked away. Her fearful neighbours huddled inside their own homes, reassuring themselves that all was well now that the house of death was burned away.

Whether they feared God or Death or Pestilence or the wild thoughts of a woman who had lost all she owned and held dear in the world is not known.

Bride took to the roads after that, staying nowhere for any length of time. She spent a day here and a day there. Her spinning skills were welcomed among the people she met as some living crept back into the world once more and people began to need more than subsistence food in their lives.

Bride joined that great tribe of walking people who traversed the roads of Ireland long ago. Always walking on, never stopping long anywhere, mindful that something that might be on the road behind them might catch up. Mindful that happiness and reunion perhaps awaited them at the end of the long, long, road.

It is said by some that Bride lived to more than ninety years of age. Wherever she is laid to rest it is not in Dunquin graveyard for no sod was ever again lifted from that grave, according to the late Mícheál Ó Dubhsláine who first narrated the story in *Inisvickillane* his fine book of the area.

20

Rose of love

His parents thought Hughie was something special, that he was destined for greatness. For that reason, they kept Hughie apart from other children at play so he could grow into his destiny.

Children attended national school up to sixth class, then, after which they were old enough to make their own way, by law. Some took up children's jobs in shops and industry, some went to secondary schooling in the arts and some went to vocational schools to learn a trade. A few stayed at primary school for an extra year that was known as seventh book.

Hughie stayed on in seventh class on his own. On the cusp of puberty, he was given to unpredictable rushes of blood through his scrawny body. He blushed a lot at unpredictable moments. His parents thought it a sign and waited patiently for the next manifestation of the Truth that their son was a living saint.

Hughie's parents ran a small necessities shop in the front room of their terraced house, as did many impoverished families. They thought it a fine idea that Hughie should assist them as shop manager. His schooling in mental arithmetic allowed him to swiftly calculate the likely profit in selling two bruised apples at a reduced price before closing time and the end of their usefulness to anyone.

Hughie tried to break away from their stifling embrace; but nobody would employ him for fear his fawning parents would follow him to his place of employment. When he travelled the five miles to the next town nobody would give him work there because he was not from that place.

Such historic arguments passed Hughie by, for he fell in love for the first time ever in that town.

He managed to secure a few week's work in one establishment measuring out flour and the like in the back room of a general store. While he remained out of sight the shopkeeper assured him he could stay as long as he satisfied requirements.

It was while he measured and filled and stacked and poured in the twilight-world of dust, sacks, boxes, crates, vats and vessels that circumstances took a turn that would see Hughie's life course set forever.

He met and fell in love with Rita who had red Irish hair and blue eyes and white freckled skin. She smiled at him and when she saw how embarrassed he was she smiled so sweetly that he fell in love with her so deeply and irrevocably he was no use for anything else.

Which is why he was dismissed on Friday. All he had done for the week was moon over Rita with the gorgeous hair. The more he mooned the less work he completed for his employer.

Many a man has been driven mad by passion; many more by unfulfilled desire. And since Hughie at 15 years of age was at the threshold of such mysterious forces, and had neither job nor prospects, the girl's father, Hughie's employer, forbade Rita to see him at all.

Hughie went home with no job and little to do beyond standing behind the counter of his parent's little shop waiting for someone to come in. Rita went off to America when she was 18 years old. She wrote to him once a year, on her birthday, and then not at all.

Uneventful years passed during which Hughie grew into young manhood and his parents died within a month of one another during a bitter long winter. If they were disappointed that Hughie, their Golden Son, had not yet achieved greatness they had the grace not to say much about it before they slipped out of his life.

Once they were gone, Hughie took even less care of himself. Sales in the shop dwindled away to nothing at all. No customers came in to chat and with nobody to speak to at night, either, Hughie lapsed deeper into himself, only attending the local cinema once in a while when he heard talk there was an interesting film showing.

Until one evening he went to the cinema to see a film with an actress new to him in it. She was called Rita Hayworth, the huge posters announced.

He was friends with everyone in a general way as people who live in the same small town are; but he had no particular pal. It was no matter, everyone had their favourite seat in the rundown cinema. They clung to these seats as much as if they were at home in front of the crackling fire in the hearth for all treated the cinema as their living room.

Hughie laughed at some of the ribald jokes he heard from former classmates and even thought up his own contribution but did not manage to call them out to the others.

He was so distracted and was not therefore prepared for the shock that was to come. When Rita Hayworth met his eyes from the big screen, Hughie believed she was looking at him. She was the spitting image of his own Rita from the shop, or at least what he remembered of her, for it was a few calendar years since those glorious days, those moments in an arrested life.

Rita of the laughing smile, the young girl not yet exposed to the world. But if it was her, then his Rita had grown away from him. He watched in horrified admiration as she dealt with two male lovers as only Rita Hayworth could. It was to be his first and only cinematic experience of this woman in her raw prime. His blood ran warm; his hair tingled along his scalp and may have stood on end, though nobody could see it in the surrounding darkness that existed beneath a fog of cigarette smoke.

Afterwards, on his way home through the calling voices, he felt light-headed and delirious even though he realised a chapter of his life had closed for evermore. Rita was gone. He could not follow.

Hughie stopped going out at all after that night. He took no interest in his appearance and was not overly concerned whether he washed himself at all.

While his body grew older and thinner, Hughie fell into bad health and was taken to hospital many times for resuscitation as one year followed another.

Every time he went into hospital, good people emptied Hughie's abode of the detritus of a male hermit's cave.

His parents' shop was long since closed down. The State supported the near-destitute Hughie with a weekly income under one heading, or, another. He lived on that without bothering about employment by anyone else.

Each time he returned home from hospital Hughie went back to his old ways try as the good people might to show him basic cleanliness by example. Neither his body nor his dwelling were cleaned while Hughie was in residence. In time he grew old enough to be admitted to day care attention but even then other senior citizens refused to call into the daycare centre at dinnertime when he was there because of the odour wafting from his clothes and body.

He was eventually asked to stay at home. Food was brought to him by a rotating team of volunteers. Other than that he lived alone.

Solitary days passed during which Hughie had fewer and fewer people to converse with through the long hours of a day or night. It seemed he was marking the days until he would breathe no more.

Then, he was taken away on a stretcher once more. He was at death's door without having achieved his parent's anticipated greatness.

Only this time he was transformed in that mad strange way that sometimes happens when a person has almost nodded off and are brought back again as if by an external force.

For Hughie met a nurse who was from America and who looked like his lost love should have looked. That is, she looked like Rita from the next town might have if she had she not gone off and became Rita Hayworth and been on a huge white screen for all to see and no privacy or pride or self respect about it. Rosetta, the nurse from Brooklyn was a great listener and Hughie told her all.

On being admitted to hospital, Hughie was deloused and washed down, as usual. On leaving, he was fitted out with a tweed jacket, cord trousers and brown brogues that had been donated to the hospital. In his buttonhole he sported a flower of the day and a comb in his pocket that he used to slick back his dampened hair before he went anywhere.

And he shaved most days.

He attended all the senior citizens gatherings with everyone else and was asked for his considered opinion on many matters. And because he was slow of speech, from lack of practice, people new to the town believed him to be a wise man who had simply withdrawn from society for some contemplation.

His new friend Rosetta the nurse even called to see him in his spick and span house once every month.

Passing neighbours were astonished to hear laughter from the house for the first time in living memory. Some were uneasy at the strangeness of it all.

Then in the first week of September when Hughie had not appeared for a few days some thought he had returned into his own madness. A virtuous teenager volunteered to break in the back door to see what he could see.

They found Hughie's body sitting before the cold fireplace in a soft armchair with a flower in his buttonhole and a picture of Rita Hayworth in his hand. People laughed at his dead handhold of a pouting Rita Hayworth kneeling in a lace nightgown gazing backwards at the beholder.

News of his passing ran through the community with some saying they thought he had died many years earlier and others recalling moments in his sad life as anecdotes in the life of Hughie.

They buried him with his parents in their three-person grave. The American nurse was not there: why, nobody could say for sure. Grief, some said. Others said her lover had called her home to Brooklyn.

Hughie was almost eighty years old when he went to ground. Neighbours followed his coffin to the old graveyard where he was buried.

Strangely enough, every year since, fresh flowers are placed on his grave on the anniversary of his birth.

And they come from America each time.

The card says they are From Rita.

21

Three choices

At times, it was like a relay race of argument in the home of Enda and Kathleen. It was entirely the fault of Enda, according to Kathleen, who told him so, long and loudly. However, Enda did not agree it was his fault and responded in like manner.

Other times, all fault belonged to Kathleen, according to Enda, who happily pointed out her failings to her in detail, and invited his wife to agree with him on their veracity.

No day passed without argument. Many who knew them took sides. These interlopers declared that many of the arguments were because the warring couple had no children to show example to in respect for others.

One day, they had a devil of a row and Enda got as mad as could be. Though in truth, if he was placed on the witness stand and asked to say which barbed jibe had struck him so deeply, he would not have been able to say. It was enough that he had come to the end of his patience for him to take the next step.

He summoned up his sense of self and in a loud clear voice told Kathleen to clear out of the place and not to come back any more. He made his announcement in booming tones that were followed by a silence not heard in their mutual abode for many years.

On a technicality, the house was left to him by his late parents. He was the legal and sole owner, even if Kathleen had made her home in it for many years, declared Enda.

Kathleen said he could not tell her to leave, at all. Enda said he meant everything he said and she should get out of his home. Well, in that case, Kathleen said she would go. To make matters more final, and to end it forever, Enda told her that he did not care if she never came back.

Kathleen responded with unsure certainty: 'I don't care to stay with you one day more. I will have a happier life without you; all my days had been unhappy in your company and anything is better than this arguing and fighting with such a person as you. I deserve better and am entitled to much more out of life.'

To which Enda responded not at all.

Kathleen took her time to collect up as many goods as she believed she owned. She said she was bringing them with her, each and every one of them.

But, when two people live as one for a long time, it is in truth hard to say who owns what even if a single owner could be decided upon.

Enda saw Kathleen marking many items he would need himself if he was to carry on the household as a single occupant. He became determined he would not lose out in the matter of property.

He told his soon-to-be-departing spouse that she would have to leave without some items. Kathleen argued that what was hers was hers. He was entitled to what was his but to no more than that.

Enda said: 'That is correct and proper but what you are taking is not yours to take.'

And so another argument wound its way through the day until they retired to bed in exhaustion.

The next morning, when it might be expected that yesterday's words would fade away with a night's repose, they returned to the sundering of their joint household.

Enda mended his hand from the night before when he said that Kathleen could take just three items with her, with his leave.

'You can take away any three things you like best in the place,' he declared. 'You can do so with my blessing no matter which of us brought these items into the household in the first place, nor how long they have been here.'

In this he felt quite magnanimous. After all, Kathleen had been his wife for a great many years and she was entitled to some recognition for this.

She asked him if he meant what he said about her three wishes?

He said he did mean it; she could have whatever she wanted; but no more than three items, that was her limit. He would not yield on that, he was certain of it.

Kathleen looked about at the belongings she had selected from their life together. Truth to tell, a lot of it was ephemera she had earmarked because she knew Enda really liked that piece and she wanted to take it to vex him. She had not even considered what she would do with it. Most likely it would be discarded, or burnt in the red flames of the fire that set everything to ash.

Kathleen put aside all other thoughts so she could consider which three items she would take with her. It was not an easy decision. Should she take the essentials of a household so she could start up again somewhere else? Should she take whatever Enda could not do without, the better to aggravate him and to intrude on his peace of mind when she was no longer there to argue with him? Or should she take that which was light and valuable and easier to carry away and which would benefit her most in the time ahead?

She had brought a dowry with her to this marriage, so she was entitled to that, she reasoned. That was fair. So, she went to the tea caddy beneath the bed and drew out what money was there. It was her treasure saved up over the years against a want that might confront them. Enda might suspect she had her own small amount of money put aside for a bothersome day; but it never came into the household reckoning. So she would take that with her and think no more of it.

Then there was her second choice. It was an easy one for a woman without a child to clutch at her skirts seeking attention. A travelling man had asked her one day if he might leave his dog with her? He expected to be arrested for some minor matter, he said. The trouble was that in his past he had been imprisoned for youthful adventures, so it was likely that he would be given a sentence in prison this time. He did not want Luci his dog to be put down or locked up in a dog pound, so he wondered if Kathleen would be so decent as to give her bed and board until he returned, when he would pay her whatever the reckoning might be for the dog's lodging.

Kathleen agreed and weathered argument from Enda when he saw the traveller's dog ensconced beside the fireplace. Luci was rolled up in a ball watching the dancing flame in peace and comfort. She showed no sign of wanting to return to the road with anyone. Her master somehow or another never returned to claim her as his own, whether he was jailed or not.

So now, Kathleen had two things she was allowed to take away with her. She was happy. She had enough money to keep her going and she had a dog to keep her company and to watch out for strangers.

She told Enda what she was taking with her. He agreed to that and wondered what her third choice might be?

It is a fact that women of the mid-twentieth century were strong in their bearing for everything had to be prepared from basics, from cooking to baking to keeping the home fire tended and making the beds; every day.

Men were strong as well, for almost everything in life at that time required some physical strength. Enda was as strong as life required of him. But, on this day, he was more than surprised to find himself hoisted up onto his wife's back.

One minute he was standing there, the next he was piggyback on Kathleen's back.

He did not know what was the matter with her, at all. He scrambled down off her back and asked what did she mean at all by doing as she did?

'You gave me leave to take away three things out of the place, the three things I like best,' she answered firmly. 'You are one of the three things I like best and I am bringing you with me.'

When he heard her talking like that, Enda saw that whatever faults his wife had, she was very fond of him at the back of it all.

He then said he was sorry for what he had done and said. It wasn't hard for her to say that she was also sorry for all she had said.

And from that day on, they lived as a married couple should. They were so polite to one another that others avoided their never-ending civility after a while. And, to crown it all a lovely round child was born to them within a year, once they were relaxed in themselves and the arguments faded away.

And they were all as happy as the day was long.

That's at least according to an account of the matter collected in 1935 from storyteller James White in Foulksmills, County Wexford by John Butler, a local collector of story, and held in the Irish Folklore Collection for all to see.

22

Silver shoes

When you fall in love with a man steeped in the art of black magic you know not what may happen to you, or, to him. He may even change shape and disappear forever, leaving you wondering what is to become of you and your love in the echoing days and times that follow.

For black magic and the powers it unleashes are not for the faint-hearted. It is not a frivolous parlour game to while away a long summer's evening while shadows creep slowly across the manicured grassland of your fine home.

Eleanor Butler, daughter of James, 2nd Earl of Ormonde in the 14th century, married the 24-year-old Gearóid Iarla, Earl Gerald, who was some three years her senior. Though their marriage was an arranged one of land and prestige between powerful families, they became husband and wife and to their own surprise lovers and lifelong friends. They remained steadfast throughout their married life until age slowed their step. By then, the great challenges of life had been met.

The family prospered for in addition to being a poet and a great leader of his people and skilful in the use of weapons and almost unbeatable in warfare and government Gearóid was a practitioner of the black arts.

People whispered he could change into whatever shape he pleased, at any time, go anywhere he wished and appear where he was least expected.

Eleanor was aware her husband had this power, and often asked to be shown some of his secrets. But, he never would grant her wish to see him in another form, lest his power be lessened.

She wanted particularly to see him in some strange shape, other than a human outline. But, fearing catastrophe, he put her off on one pretence or another, time after time.

Nonetheless, Eleanor had perseverance; and on one eventful evening at the closing of his days, when his will to resist had lessened, Gearóid was unable to withstand her campaign.

On a summer's evening, in their older years, when cooler air replaced the suffocating heat of day, Eleanor engaged with Gearóid in the drawing room of their great house. They sat together in matching chairs facing outwards, the better to see the calming of the day. They argued mildly over nothing at all as only seasoned couples know how.

Shadows crept across fields spreading a dappled shroud over the land. In the distance, excited calls of children swimming in the tumbling river grew faint when tiredness crept through young bodies.

Once more, Eleanor begged Gearóid to show her what he could do in black magic. This time, he relented, though had she known the consequences she would have made her tongue as still as her body in the high-backed quilted chair.

It was a moment she was not sure she wanted to reach now that it had arrived. Sometimes, she reflected, trying and striving is more enjoyable than realising the ambition.

She watched her lover, her husband, the father of their five children, make himself absolutely still and as straight as the depredations of many battles through his life on his body would allow.

His fine chiselled face in silhouette and stillness made her heart give a little flicker just as it had done when first her eyes rested on Gearóid Iarla, her beloved husband.

He was a powerful and a rich man and liked to dress in high fashion. He wore this evening a vertical costume that covered the left half of his body in fawn, and the right half in red, as was the custom of the day for people of property and wealth.

His tunic, shoulder cape, hose and shoes were finished in different hues of fawn and red.

A golden brooch held his tunic in place. A gold belt sat low on his hips, emphasising the line of the 63-year-old warrior's body.

On his feet were poulaine shoes with long, narrow pointed toes, the height of 14th century fashion. While she admired his dress sense, it was the last time Eleanor was to see him so clothed.

Gearóid spoke very little except to say to Eleanor that if she took the least fright while he was out of his natural form, he would not recover it before many generations of their descendants were deceased and under the ground in their own right.

Eleanor said she would not be a fit wife for Gearóid Iarla if she could be so easily frightened. Let him but gratify her in this wish, she said, and he'd see what a hero she was herself.

So, on this beautiful summer evening, as they were sitting in their grand drawing-room, he turned his face away from her, and muttered some words in so low a voice that Eleanor was unable to catch them so she could repeat them, at any other time, in any other place.

To her everlasting surprise and shock, and in a moment, Gearóid Iarla was clear and clean out of sight in their drawing-room. Eleanor was alone, no other person was in that room with her.

In place of her husband and father of their five children, a sole, if lovely, goldfinch flew about the high ceiling. Thinking the bird had flown in by accident Eleanor turned her attention to assisting its exit from the room.

She saw in the blur of movement that he was of colours red, white, and black and his wings were banded in brilliant yellow that caught the fascination of the eye as he flew about.

Realising who the goldfinch was in that moment of clarity that transforms a moment, his lady, as courageous as she thought herself, was startled. But she held her own, especially when he came and perched on her shoulder, and whistled the most delightful tune she had ever heard and shook his wings, and put his little beak to her lips.

Now, he flew in circles round her head and played hide and go seek with his lady. Then, he flew into the garden, and flew back again, and lay down in her lap as if asleep: and when she thought he was dead to the world he hopped up and flew around some more, making her laugh with delight.

When the sport had lasted long enough to satisfy both, he took one flight more into the open air to finish what had been a unique and enchanting and enchanted evening. Eleanor flopped back into her chair and waited to see what might happen next.

The room was still while he was away, though that was not for long; for he was on his return as fast as his little wings would carry him. Now, though, he was flying for his life.

He flew right into his lady's arms. She laughed uncertainly, though she knew in her core that something was amiss and tragedy was about to present.

Into awareness came realisation, for the next moment a fierce hawk flew into the room in deathly pursuit of the goldfinch.

Lady Eleanor gave a loud scream, though there was no need for it, for the wild bird came in like an arrow, and struck against a mahogany table with such force that life was dashed out of it, on the instant.

In shock, she turned from the marauder's quivering body to where the goldfinch had been just an instant before, but on neither goldfinch nor Gearóid Iarla did she ever lay eyes again.

Eleanor searched all corners of the room. She hoped the goldfinch was to be found somewhere, even if injured. She would nurse it back to full health, no matter how long it took. When her exploration of the room proved fruitless, Eleanor went into the world beyond the living-room to continue the search. She might seek all she wished; for her search was in vain.

That room was to become forever associated with the disappearance of her one true husband.

Though she lived to be as old as it was possible to live in those days, and she passed away at 66 years of age, an old woman, in 1404, just four years later, for each of those days she searched for her husband in vain for she was never to find him.

As for Gearóid Iarla, it is said that once every seven years the Earl rides on a stallion around the Curragh of Kildare, or the shore of Lough Gur, for it is said he never lost his supernatural skills. Though he could not return to his home in human form because of what happened when Eleanor cried out.

The shoes of his favourite horse are made of silver and were half an inch thick when he disappeared.

When the shoes are worn as thin as a cat's ear, Gearóid Iarla will be restored to the society of living men, it is said.

As for Eleanor, his wife, it seems her love took flight that summer's evening never to return as far as any mortal man can report.

But who is to say what way love found to re-unite two playful lovers?

Perhaps, perhaps.

For, armed with his skill in magic Gearóid Iarla was a force to be reckoned within this world, or, in one close by.

He may have vanished into myth and story, long ago, but his memory remains, as present and as vital as ever he was.

23

The hunted fawn

From the safety of long trailing grasses a solitary deer watched the weary hunters of the Fianna make their way home from a day of barefoot running after the fleetest of animals. The hunt was led by their chieftain, Fionn Mac Cumhaill.

Their home fort, their dún, lay ahead of them in the setting sun. Long shadows raced to greet them even while the heat of day shimmered into a pleasant evening breeze.

A Fianna hunt was long and arduous. On this evening, the bearers of dead animals changed their burden from shoulder to shoulder to ease bone tiredness.

Though the warriors be weary and the hunt at an end, the hunting hounds were ever alert for strange scents. Two slipped away towards the hidden fawn.

She watched the oncomers in momentary stillness before whisking herself away across the long swaying meadow jumping swiftly with feet together putting distance between her and danger with each bound.

The weary warriors looked to Fionn who turned to his personal hounds, Bran and Sceolán, who awaited his command. He looked to the distant quarry and nodded his head. With skidding paws, the hounds were soon away after the fawn.

Surprisingly, she fled not away, but, towards their own dún, yet on arrival there she led them on under low-branched trees, by lake shores, through strong currents, past ruins of old forts, until all but Fionn fell away. Even Bran and Sceolán were slowing when the pursued deer ceased her flight.

Finally, she turned to face them and tremblingly sank down to rest. She seemed resigned to her fate while she awaited their arrival.

To the surprise of all and against character Bran and Sceolán frolicked around the fawn, like young excited suitors, not at all like the grizzled hounds they were. They licked her face and neck and limbs in turn, first Bran, then Sceolán, one after the other, then both together.

Though he was realistic about life and death, for such considerations were a matter of daily survival for the most part, Fionn thought to kill so gentle a beast was not the correct path to follow.

Something about her demeanour caused a pleasant flutter to sound inside his chest. The hounds came to heel on his low command. When he walked away from the deer they followed in his wake.

Fionn's young life had seen him moving silently through the world, staying ahead of his slain father's enemies who were intent on killing him as his father's heir. Others would not hear the soft swish of grass as the fawn followed on, yet he did. She never closed, never lenghtened the space between them, but maintained the same distance in their wake.

Bran and Sceolán fell back to walk beside her.

The dún guardians looked down with some disbelief at the unlikely procession that approached. They saw their warrior chieftain draw near, one great wolfhound by his side and further back the other hound walking gently by the side of a hesitant fawn whose lifeless form should even now be thrown across the strong shoulders of Fionn.

When all were safely inside the fort, Fionn turned away to enter his chambers. The fawn settled down in the open where she could see the doorway. Evening came on while she waited and waited, though many wondered at this fawn sitting on the ground inside the fort none thought to bother her.

That night, inside the great hall, tales of heroism and bravado and mighty feats were recounted by those who had been on the hunt. Those who had not been there challenged the accounts, and so a battle of claim and denial raged around Fionn who took no part in the war of words.

In the huge fireplace before them burning logs settled in for the long night.

By and by, voices fell to a pleasant hum as camaraderie overcame dissension. Nonetheless, an unexpected murmur caused Fionn to turn his head to see what was afoot. He saw a slim woman of fair features and rich dress approach his chair. He had not seen her before. He would remember such a woman in his household. Without doubt.

In a voice as soft as a fawn's skin she declared herself to be the hunted quarry of the day.

An astonished Fionn arose. He could not speak. He offered his hand to her. Their fingertips brushed for the first time in soft trill. He led her to an empty sugán chair on the other side of the high wide fireplace to his. She sat gently.

Her name, she said, was Sadbh. The sound from her lips was like the soughing of a breeze on the warm hillside. Hearing it and seeing her smiling at him, Fionn fell immediately in love.

She told the company she was under a spell when Bran and Sceolán had reached her. For refusing the unwelcome advances of the druid Feardorcha, he had turned her into a deer and for three years she endured a wild deer's life in a far away place.

One day, a friendly slave told her if she was once within the fortress of the Fianna, then any power that Feardorcha had over her would be at an end. So, she came into Fionn's home territory where Bran and Sceolán came on her.

If Fionn's warriors were surprised at this story of transformation it was nothing to the reaction of their chieftain, for the lovestruck Fionn in the months that followed went to neither battle nor chase.

He was lost to all except his gentle Sadbh and she to him.

Neither were able to breathe, almost, in the company of one another. They were inseparable; where one was, there was the other.

It would have remained so until the high hills were worn down from summer rain except invaders from the north landed in the bay beside the Hill of Oaks. It being the bounden duty of the Fianna to confront such raiders, Fionn led his warriors to do battle. They were away for seven days, during which they mercilessly disposed of the attackers.

On the eighth day, Fionn crossed the plain below his fort with long strides so as to shorten the distance. At the fort, he wondered that his love was not atop the earthen mound awaiting his return.

While the other dwellers of the fort rushed out to greet their chief everywhere Fionn looked he saw great sadness on every face. He asked where his beloved Sadbh was, for foreboding grew within him.

His home guards begged him not to blame her, nor them, for what had happened.

They said that while the invaders were falling beneath his sword, at the Hill of Oaks, there appeared before the fort his very likeness with the fetches of Bran and Sceolán by his side. The occupiers thought they heard the Diord Fionn war cry sounding from the lips of Fionn. Once heard, the cry made those wounded and in travail forget their pain.

Sadbh in her excitement at their return ran down the pass within the fort, rushed through the gates; without an ear to entreaty or command. She said she must go and meet her protector, her lover, the father of their unborn infant.

Within a few moments she was away from the fort and in the arms of the phantom Fionn.

But, just as quickly, the following guards saw her start back with a scream. The form that a moment ago she so happily embraced drew itself up to a great height and struck her with a hazel wand. In an instant, a gentle, slender trembling doe was on the plain once more, where the human Sadbh stood not a moment before.

Many times she sprang towards safety, but was seized by the throat and pulled by her tormentor at every turn.

Though the fort's guardians rushed forward intent on fierce fight, neither woman, nor hind, nor sorcerer, were to be seen when they arrived, though the guards clearly heard the rapid beating of fleeing feet on the hard plain.

If they heard it clearly, each pursuer named a different quarter from which the noise was coming, all in direct conflict with one another.

But Sadbh was gone.

For seven years from that day, Fionn and everyone he knew explored every remote corner of the land in search of his beloved Sadbh. They searched everywhere she might be and everywhere she might not be. They searched in the usual places and they searched in the unusual places. Then they searched all over again. To no avail.

One day, many years later and long past his day of loss, Fionn was hunting on the side of Benbulben on the western side of the country. He and his companions heard a terrific clamour among the chasing dogs before them. It was mostly coming from a hidden defile in the land which took them a moment to reach.

On breathless arrival, they discovered the howling hounds were surrounding a small child, a boy. He was of noble features though naked, except for long hair that covered him from head to foot. He stood within the baying circle of hunting dogs, with no sign of fear. Unlike the other hounds, Bran and Sceolán fawned on him. They licked him with slavering tongues. They seemed to have forgotten their master, Fionn.

The boy was brought home by Fionn and the others to their great dún. He ate and drank in their company, and he became as one of them in the time that followed.

A wondering Fionn often considered the boy's features. He fancied he saw the sweet countenance of Sadbh in them. He hoped the boy was her child but until the child could speak Fionn was content to await the child's telling of what he knew. Though it took a while and he learnt many other things besides, as soon as the boy's tongue mastered human speech he gave his account.

He and a hind whom he tenderly loved, and who sheltered him and tended to him, lived among hills, deep glens, streams, by rocks, and in dark woods.

In summer, he lived on fruits and roots. In winter, he found food left for him in a sheltered cave.

A dark man came very so often as the boy recalled fearfully, and spoke sometimes in soft and tender tones, sometimes loud and threatening to the hind if she had not already hidden from him. She always shrank away with fear in her face and limb. He always departed in great anger.

The last time the boy beheld the hind, the dark man angrily struck her with a hazel wand upon which she was obliged to follow him, still looking back at the boy and calling piteously in protest.

The boy said he responded in rage and sorrow, but had not the power to move for he too was under a spell. He struggled and he struggled and from struggling so long, he fell on the ground quite insensible; where the hounds of the Fianna discovered him.

Of Sadbh there was never any trace found though Fionn and the Fianna searched until none of them remained in the land of the living anymore.

The boy took his place with his father's people and in sorrow at the loss of Sadbh and in joy at the discovery of their son, Fionn named the child Oisín.

Oisín was to become famous in his own right as a lover, storyteller, poet and the subject of more great adventures.

24

The woman who married the wrong man

The beauty of Bessy Keogh was the cause of a matrimonial journey by the son of her employer that resulted in an unforeseen union of two unrelated people. It happened this way.

Mick Jones's mother decided it was time for her son to be married. But not to a servant of theirs.

For Bessy was a servant girl. And a young farmer should marry land and money. She acknowledged that Bessy was a decent girl and pretty with it, but a servant nonetheless. Mrs Jones was a widow and very particular about who might be allowed in around the place to succeed her in God's good time when she went below ground for a well-earned rest.

Michael, as his mother insisted on calling him, was a stout-built man. He was unsurpassed in his enthusiasm for work; but was a bad hand at courting women. He would tremble if left near one unaccompanied by someone who could converse with women in a way that he could not. He could talk to farm animals all day and make sensible conversation but was speechless if he had to address a woman on matters unrelated to husbandry.

His skin would redden more than usual for a countryman. His tongue was often in danger of being bitten through by his chattering teeth in such encounters.

Acknowledging this, Mrs Jones resolved to send Mick on a courting expedition from their native Wexford into the nearby county of Carlow.

The custom was that a go-between would accompany the would-be-suitor. This character was called a Blackman in Irish society of the time.

Mick's appointed companion was a lively fidget of a neighbouring farmer whom Mrs Jones thought to be a good judge of a potential bride. His name was Richard O'Connor.

She had a particular quarry in mind, a Miss Catherine Murphy.

Having been well briefed by the mother, the pair set off on a Tuesday morning in July with a fair and a warm wind at their back.

Mick said he had stopped a few times at the Murphy home on cattle-buying expeditions. Richard said he had been on the spot on a couple of occasions himself, for reasons now lost to time. All seemed propitious for matchmaking.

The men rode on horseback until they came to Catherine's snug little home. It was as neat a holding as could be found in many hours journeying in any direction.

The walls had been whitewashed at Corpus Christi and reflected the sun well on this day. All fences were in order, all animals were where they should be. A smell of fresh bread met them halfway up the hill. It seemed they were expected.

They were greeted by Catherine's parents on the doorstep and invited indoors, according to Patrick Kennedy of Wexford who made a study of this story not long after it played out.

Ensconced in the house and facing the fire that burned away even though it was the month of July, they chattered away about farming, the weather and their neighbours so as not to have to discuss marriage before Mick, who was already shaking quietly on his hard chair.

The men were dressed much alike. They wore their best courting clothes: coats of brown, top-boots, cassimere breeches, and formal hats, though they took off their hats when they came indoors.

Matters proceeded well and badly at the same time. Whereas Richard was always ready for a laugh or a smile; and let nothing escape without some genial observation, Mick stared ahead with the dogged, disturbed look of a man that knew the ship arriving with his life's treasure had foundered on the sharp rocks of chance.

Before they left home, Mick had tried to slither away from the job in hand.

'I'd rather have a quiet wedding with poor Bessy Keogh, than all this bother, what with clipping my hair, shaving and bleeding myself, and putting on a cravat that half chokes me.'

His mother ignored her son's bleatings.

On the journey, he suggested that Richard, being his Blackman, should find something for Mick to talk about as well as fomenting ould chat for himself. He even threatened to take Richard's life if he left him a minute alone with the young woman.

To which Richard replied, amiably enough, that he would have no objection to changing places with his companion. In a lightly mocking voice, he said it would not be a great hardship to sit down by a fine young woman, like Miss Murphy, and praise her beauty, and her fine silken hair, and tell her that no one was to be seen between here and there to compare with her, and that she was never out of a man's thoughts waking or sleeping, for she was a well-featured young woman of just twenty-four years of age. and looking well on it.

'I'd rather marry Bessy for I'm sure poor Bessy likes me, at least,' said Mick.

Bessy cried when he was leaving on the matchmaking trip and hid her face when his mother came in so she would not see her damp cheeks. This he told to Richard on the road. But Richard did not seem to be listening to him at all.

'She can read and write a good hand, she's a good seamstress and housekeeper, said Mick. 'Hers is a respectable family, though they are reduced in circumstance.'

When she'd be carrying a heavy basket, he'd take one side, he said. 'I hold up the skein of wool for her when she winds the snaking wool into a ball. I drove home the cows for her. I put in a soft word when her mistress scolded her. I even bought a bit of a silk ribbon for her, an odd time, at the market.'

By contrast, this Catherine, while she was civil enough any time Mick stopped at the house had a way of chilling a witticism or a compliment, before he could open his mouth to make it, Mick muttered truculently.

He noticed that while Catherine's soft white hand was steady enough in his own great big paw when they shook hands, it faltered a little when she presented her hand to Richard, whatever that was about.

A dinner was served up of floury potatoes, bacon, and cabbage. Mick was placed beside Catherine, as might be expected. True to form, he made a bags of anything he was required to do. His knife and fork were as often on the ground as in his hands, and if his plate did not hit the ground, it was entirely due to good luck.

Catherine, seeing his distress, spoke kindly to him of different matters. She expressed her great pleasure at seeing him as her guest. She pressed him to eat heartily, and to put shyness aside for the duration of the meal.

Mick struggled his way through the ordeal as best he could while Richard told endless stories in which Mick was the hero. Dinner being over, Catherine's mother suggested that Catherine might show their visitor the near parts of the farm.

While they did so, Catherine's mother and her husband, and Richard, took seats by the big chimney, and smoked pipes, to arrange the marriage portion.

After a good deal of talk, back and forth, they came to terms. It remained only for the couple to agree on the marriage which was considered by the negotiators to be a formality.

However, Mick was not getting on very well in truth for in helping his potential bride over a low drain, he gave her left foot a good wetting. Then, her wrist was mildly sprained by a twist of his uncouth hand while assisting her across a fence which she normally passed over effortlessly on her own.

While Catherine remarked on the delightful appearance of the mountain side, with the low evening sun shining so nicely on it, Mick expressed his fears that his workmen would not be sufficiently diligent in bringing in his stock in his absence.

Aloud, he tried a few compliments he had rehearsed on the road; but they fell into the ditch as soon as he said them.

Tiring of the excruciating effort at conversation he finally cried out: 'It would be a pity for a fine woman like you to waste your time on the likes of me'.

Whatever her private considerations, Catherine disagreed with him in a few polite words, though she soon moved the discourse on to Richard.

Glad to turn away from the conversation, Mick happily sang the praises of his companion. He lauded his sound judgment, cheerfulness of disposition, real piety, and good conduct. Catherine encouraged him to tell her more.

She hinted to her suitor that though she felt a sincere kindness towards him, she did not privately consider their union in marriage would be desirable for either. A delighted Mick agreed with her.

'Did I not say the same myself only a few minutes ago?'

In which case, once the couple returned and their demeanour was read by all, the company turned to an evening of relaxation. Songs were sung, stories told, poetry well recited. The evening slowed to a natural end as all evenings will do. They retired to bed, each to their allotted space. Marriage was not discussed any more on that evening.

However, Richard was delighted when he heard of the failure of direct marriage negotiations as related to him by Mick in the privacy of their guest bedroom.

At once, his own fancy filled in a bright future of happiness in the society of a dear companion so well fitted to his own lasting love and esteem: Miss Catherine Murphy.

On the following morning, Richard stated that he could now freely say what he would have wished to say the evening before had be been a free man and allowed to speak on his own behalf.

He declared to the old couple that he had the most sincere esteem and affection for their daughter. 'I would think this the happiest journey ever made, if you would receive me into your family, with your blessing.'

Her not-altogether-surprised parents informed Catherine of this development. She responded with ever-widening smiles on the news, for she knew the feelings she had for Richard were returned in full measure.

No sooner was the news out than the two men swapped places.

Richard walked out with a beaming Catherine on his arm while Mick acted in the manner of the settlement with her parents.

That agreement made, all united in persuading Mrs. Jones to allow her son to please himself in the choice of wife. She gave way after a short siege.

Mick led Bessy to the priest's parlour, where formal arrangements were made for posting the banns some Sundays before the marriage.

They were married shortly afterwards.

Mick did manage to hit his head off the lectern and missed giving the bride the first kiss of her married life, that honour being stolen from him by a lively old man from the next parish.

As for the union of Richard O'Connor and Miss Catherine Murphy: well Mick and Bessy were the guests of honour at that wedding and were entirely happy with their life together.

As was Catherine, the woman who happily married the wrong man.

25

The prescient writing of a snail

A young mother suckled her baby on a slow-moving canal boat on its tedious journey across the Irish midlands on a warm day in May.

Below decks, sweating strangers crowded together united stoically for the length of this journey. Grace, the young mother, was married to Liam, an older father, who was standing at the rail looking for a particular spot to ask that the boat be halted. And all because of the thatched writing of a snail.

In the event, when the horse stopped of its own accord, knowing its own business best, Liam took their baby David from Grace and pushed his way through the milling crowd. Grace followed him onto the bank of the canal.

She soon retrieved her child from its father's clumsy embrace and wrapped her cloak around the child. She picked her steps carefully in his wake, lest she stumble on the dimly seen track leading away from the canal.

Before long, they came to a turf hut some distance away from the canal and its noisy travellers. Liam, in the lead, came up to Poll the old woman who lived here, for the second time in his life. She had changed not a whit, since he first made his solitary way to this place.

Poll, whose age no one has ever been able to discover, lived in this hut. It was also her place of business.

Gazing inside, the curious Grace saw that she had a wooden spinning wheel by the door. Liam had already explained that she seldom turned it, except when the priest passed her dwelling and looked in, suspiciously.

The priest questioned whether she had a real means of support, other than the telling of nonsense to those willing to part with some coins for her vision of their future.

Poll knew the value of appearances to upright citizens who listened to the priest's opinions more than they should. She must be seen to live by something, so she spun the wheel when she heard footsteps approaching her den.

For all that and to spite the puffing clergyman, she stroked a black green-eyed cat while she held court. She pretended to be unaware that black green-eyed cats were held in superstitious dread by the unschooled masses.

This dwelling of hers was raised in the form of a cone to deflect the worst travails of foul weather coming off the unprotected bog. Grass and wild flowers sprouted from its roof. A trench encircled the turf hut, draining bog water away. To ensure that all visitors met Poll from the same direction, a narrow strip of bog oak was laid across the trench for access.

Inside was a single room. It was hard to see or breathe in the room, but Poll seemed oblivious to it all. Indeed, the place was warm and dry, for though the rain could enter in one or two places, it could also run out as quickly as it came in.

The hut was furnished with a bed, three stools to sit on, and a red dresser containing crockery and some dusty green bottles. Poll told Grace they contained only a sup of eye-water, a wash for the hives, and a cure for the chin-cough.

The scent of whiskey came from the spirits that were the foundation of every cure, she assured them. The herbs were sent by the grace of God, and were gathered by herself while she fasted from food under the beam of the full moon.

On his first visit here, Liam had gone to Poll to seek insight on the sort of wife he was likely to marry, not having set eyes on Grace up to then, though they were now parents to the child they carried with them.

Poll told him then to go back to where he came from on that day, and to wait until May eve, the night before Lá Bealtaine, or, Mayday.

He was to place the garter of his right stocking around his left knee, and his left garter around his right. He was to tie his thumbs in a cross with a piece of peeled rowan-tree. When that was done, Liam was to go to the church abbey-yard, and take up the third snail he met there under an ivy leaf. He was to bring it home, and place it between two plates. He was to position the twist of the rowan-tree bark on top of the plate.

On May morning, after early sunrise, he was to lift up the plate, and whatever was written thereon would be the two letters of his future wife's name.

Though Liam could read print, he was no hand at unravelling cursive writing, neither was he proficient at deciphering it nor creating it himself. It was something the snails in the garden took pride in, he told anyone that would listen, though few would.

Liam did as he was told by Poll. He washed and cleaned and dried his two best remaining plates. He left them on the table to await the snail's arrival. He went to the churchyard and he found the snail where it was said it would be.

He took it home as carefully as possible, cupped in both calloused hands. He spoke to nobody he passed though that did not seem to discommode many of the people he met on the way.

He said a silent prayer and placed the transplanted snail on the bottom plate. He covered it with the second plate, denying himself thereafter the natural inclination to peep in at the snail to see what it was writing.

That was a restless night for a single man. He lay down on the last day of spring and arose on the first day of summer, though the turning of the season overnight did not interest Liam all that much, that year. It was the turning of the plate that interested him most.

In his excitement, he flipped the plates so swiftly that the snail fell to the floor and was crushed beneath his anxious boot. But the noble snail's work of a lifetime was done.

There it was, the name of his future wife. Liam was sure of it, though he could not read what it said, not being an expert in snail writing, he recalled for Grace, Poll, and the infant child now suckling once more, in this smoky turf hut on the Bog of Allen.

Each waited for Liam to continue.

He delayed for a moment, savouring the moment and the memory. Each woman awaited this man's continuance with forbearance born of practice.

He turned the plate one way and another to catch the light in his small cottage, he recalled, for them now. He could see the snail writing very clearly; but, as he had already said, he could not quite translate it into words that he could be sure of in the matter of a confirmed spouse.

He wondered what to do and to whom he could turn for clarification.

The name of Billy Vourney the schoolmaster came to him; a man he knew to be the soul of discretion.

So, he hurried along there holding the precious plate close to him. He was impervious to the curious glances of those he passed on the street.

He lifted up the large brass knocker on the master's door and let if fall with a heavy thud that brought Billy Vourney to the door with some alacrity fearing that a tragedy had occurred somewhere that required his attention.

Seeing who it was at the door, the mystified teacher brought Liam into the parlour at the front of the house, from where Liam could see the busy street outside through the white lace curtains. Mr Vourney closed the door of the room and sat on the other side of the table to the man with a plate in his reverential hands. The school teacher took time to listen to Liam with interest. He afforded him all the respect he believed proper.

When his visitor had spoken his piece, the master studied the plate and was silent for some time. Liam recalled this for his listeners in the hut on the Bog of Allen, as if it were important.

Master Vourney asked Liam to confirm that the snail had written the name of his future wife, or, at least her initials on the plate. Liam agreed that it was so, initials only. Liam was excited, for he knew his destiny was being realised.

The teacher placed the white plate with its snail's trail on it on the table between them. He was lost in thought for a time before he confessed that he was in an invidious position.

That Liam did not know what invidious meant was of no consequence. He nodded in a conspiratorial way. Master to apprentice. Man to man.

Master Vourney told Liam that the snail had indeed written something upon the white plate. However, if it were the initials of his future bride that were indicated, then his dilemma was that the initials were GV. His professional difficulty was that his third daughter, who was unmarried, and whose name was Grace, carried the initials GV.

Liam was at a loss as to how this created a problem. The snail had clearly written the initials of Grace Vourney. Ergo, he said to the schoolmaster, he was destined to marry Grave Vourney and that was what he would do. With her father's permission.

Looking at the slow plain features of the former Miss Grace Vourney here beside her in the hut, Poll was inclined to see why the master had deciphered the writing of the snail as accurately as he had.

And, said Liam with a flourish: 'that is why we are here today. We are here to thank you and to wish you all that you wish for yourself and to see how well your advice worked out for us.'

He shook hands with Poll, shook hands with his wife, he shook hands with his infant child and before Poll could say much more about anything, the trio were gone from her turf hut, traipsing their way back to the Royal Canal.

Poll reached up for a bottle of something while she observed Liam in the distance shake hands with the horse-man and greet the rejuvenated canal horse as an old friend, while Grace silently surveyed the boat that was to carry her onwards to the next adventure in her life.

Grace sighed deeply for the ways of the world and the writing of a snail that had brought her to this pass.

But she knew, even if Liam did not realise it yet, that their journey was to continue, and who could say what might happen?

26

Face at the window

Love between classes can have surprising consequences for the unsuspecting even many years later.

While Lord Fanshawe was ambassador at the Spanish Court under Charles II, his wife, Lady Fanshawe, was normally domiciled in Ireland.

On one occasion she elected to pay a visit to the household of Lady Honora O'Brien following an invitation that she might do so.

Lady Fanshawe duly made the journey with as much bustle and fanfare and assumed decorum as appropriate for the spouse of an ambassador on such occasions.

They were royally received at what was in reality the remaining keep of a castle. That is to say it was almost self-contained with no great castle wings fluttering around a courtyard in which to become lost, which pleased Lady Fanshawe, for she liked to be certain of her surroundings, while away.

The keep rose several stories above what had been a moat. This was now empty save for some scrawny grass and a few wandering cattle grazing the mangy sward.

Everyone contrived to believe this was a very auspicious visit of someone of importance, even if the ambassador was away on business in Spain.

The best of food was presented to the guests. Local spirits and imported wine flowed freely; a storyteller told stories and recited poetry, even composing some lines in memory of this special occasion, lines that Lady Fanshawe later asked her hostess to copy down so she might casually mention to the ambassador the high esteem in which she was held by others, especially poets in residence.

The evening rolled along in this way and if there was a reticence among locally-invited guests to fully engage with the festivity then it passed by Lady Fanshawe's increasingly warm observation of the proceedings.

Her own retinue, attuned to gossip and intrigue were aware that something was amiss; but could find neither information nor illumination from their peers-in-residence worth passing along.

All they could glean was that it was a night to remain behind closed doors once you had retired, no matter what sounds were heard or what sights were seen at windows.

Lady Fanshawe's servants and retainers knew to heed the offered advice; even if it was not specific enough to advise their good lady of such whisperings.

Lady Fanshawe, for her part, bestowed kindness on everyone who swam into her presence. She was the wife of the royal ambassador to the court of the King of Spain, after all. As such, this reception was her due. Her visit was to last but a few days; but she believed now she might stay somewhat longer. She would see.

A huge log fire threw dancing shadows all around the great room while feasting was at its height though it calmed down when the evening drew to a close and no more firing was added to the red and yellow embers.

Pitchers were not re-filled, though the drinkers no longer noticed, most having fallen asleep where they were. The storyteller led many eyelids into dreamtime. Wild dancing music gave way to soothing lullaby.

By and by, Lady Honora O'Brien asked her guest if she would care to retire to her room on the upper floor of the castle?

By which Lady Fanshawe understood it was time to retire. So she said she would indeed do so and would see everyone once more on the morrow.

Lady Honora O'Brien accompanied her guest and her servants to the highest room, at the top of what seemed to be an endless succession of stone steps.

Lady Fanshawe said she looked forward to seeing the fine view of the surrounding countryside on the morrow. If when she said this she noticed a quietness in her hostess, she took it to be some envy of her guest on her part, which was understandable.

Once Lady Fanshawe was settled, Lady Honora O'Brien withdrew with her wishes for a peaceful night.

When a servant pulled the heavy window drapes across to keep heat in the room Lady Fanshawe saw through the momentary space that a white frost covered the surrounding fields. A full moon shone that night.

One by one, Lady Fanshawe's servants also withdrew, until she was alone in a large four-poster bed with its hanging curtains pulled tight against the chill of night. Copper bed-warming pans placed beneath the upper blankets in the bed were there to ease the cold and damp of the room in such an old castle.

A new young fire burned brightly in this fireplace; sufficient fresh wood had been piled on it to sustain flickering light and heat until the occupant of the room fell asleep.

However, with the events of the evening and her almost-royal reception playing in her head she was kept from all but a fitful slumber. She tossed about in the bed seeking a spot more conducive to a night's sleep; but, if it was there, she could not locate it. In the event, Lady Fanshawe lost herself in a superficial slumber.

As she slept, the fire shadow slowed its dance in the room, for the wood had quite burned its way through. Only the occasional settling of ashes on the glowing pile of burnt embers in the grate was to be heard.

When all seemed set for a night's rest, Lady Fanshawe was disturbed in her sleep by a sound that did not fit in with the moment. At first, it was a restlessness that entered her upper ear, the lower one being well buried in the feather pillow. Then, a louder noise fully awoke her. It was more of a scratching noise. Mice, she believed somewhat irritably, wishing they would go elsewhere.

Then it became a tapping on the window of the room that she had been assured was the highest guest room in the castle. Lady Fanshawe became fully awake. All had turned chillingly cold now. She sat up, drew her knitted sleeping shawl tightly about her and listened even more carefully.

A clear tapping sounded on the window that faced out to the empty moat below. It came from behind the heavy curtain that hung between the room and the window. Of that she was absolutely certain.

Lady Fanshawe opened the curtains herself, not wishing to summon a servant lest she be dreaming and appear foolish to the lower orders. When she did, to her surprise, she beheld, by the light of the white moon, a female figure leaning against the casement, outside.

Of ghastly complexion, the woman had long red hair, and was enveloped in a white gown that fluttered about her, emphasising the contours of a shapely figure.

At this apparition Lady Fanshawe stared in horror. The form outside mouthed indistinct words in a strange wail and departed with a mournful sigh, before Lady Fanshawe quite knew what to do.

By now, Lady Fanshawe had difficulty in maintaining enough air in her own body to sustain life. She fainted, tumbling to the floor with a shish of her own night attire. There she lay, for some time, in complete silence, at first in unconsciousness, then, with returning realisation that she was not where she should be.

There being nothing else for it, she reluctantly returned to consciousness.

Still sitting on the floor, Lady Fanshawe wondered if perhaps she had not had a little too much to drink at the supper and had become somewhat light-headed as a result?

It seemed the most likely explanation. Anything else was silly. Best not to call for assistance. Best to sleep on it and see how the world appeared in the morning.

So, she climbed back into the bed after making a surreptitious inspection of the world outside the window. Nothing at all could be seen that should not be there. Surprisingly, given the circumstances, she went fast asleep while the household slumbered on as far as she could discern from deep beneath the bedcovers.

Next morning, having arisen late, Lady Fanshawe made her way to the dining hall to break her fast.

At table, and in response to a polite enquiry from Lady Fanshawe as to how her hostess had passed the night, Lady Honora O'Brien spoke in low respectful tones tinged with sorrow and sadness.

Her cousin, she said, whose ancestors once owned the castle, died in the early hours of the morning. The Banshee was heard wailing for him before his departure. Perhaps Lady Fanshawe had been disturbed in the night?

But Lady Fanshawe, admitting now that her sleep had not been interrupted by a vivid dream, said she thought she had seen a young woman who seemed to be in the full of her health, if somewhat hysterically distraught, not an old banshee.

Lady Honora O'Brien after some gentile hesitation confessed that it was not a banshee that had manifested itself, but something else entirely unique to this castle. It was the ghost of a woman seduced and murdered in the grounds by an ancestor of the gentleman who had died in the early hours.

She was of local stock and loved her man deeply, Lady O'Brien revealed quietly. So quietly did she speak that it was almost a whisper.

However, he had been playing with her and said such sweet things as she needed to hear for him to circumvent her token defences.

When she confessed she was carrying their child and the child should be recognised as legitimate and take its place in the family of its father, he dispensed with the threat to his family's good name by taking her life there and then. Once she was dead, he threw her lifeless body into the castle moat.

That death occurred beneath the window of the room where Lady Fanshawe passed the night, said her hostess. The re-appearance of this woman caused more terror to the inhabitants of the castle than those of other spirits ever could, for mingled with terrible grief was a thirst for revenge that knew no quenching.

It came as little surprise to Lady Fanshawe to hear that the murderous ancestor was subsequently thrown from his horse on the anniversary of her death. He took some weeks to expire of his coruscating injuries and he screamed the dead woman's name all the way out of this life.

Such is love misplaced, explained Lady Honora O'Brien to Lady Fanshawe who quiet soon remembered an urgent reason to take leave of Lady Honora and her demented forebears.

For there is love and there is love and Lady Fanshawe preferred her romance without complication.

27

Man in the mirror

Not so long ago, men delayed entering into marriage until they could support a home-based wife and umpteen children.

Mostly, it was because a man had to serve an apprenticeship to a profession before he could command full recompense for his labours --- man's wages. When such a man came into his maturity he often sought to marry a woman somewhat younger than himself who could bear children that would support them both in their older years.

And having lived for so long in a single state, men were not always conscious of their appearance to others.

Such a man was Mr Conaty, a lawyer who practised in the Four Courts of Dublin.

He was a skilled combatant in the courts and argued well and long for his long list of clients. However, while Conaty was known to be simpleminded and kind-hearted in his personal life away from the courts; he was also most negligent of his appearance.

His trousers drooped down, unsupported by anything but the crudest of knots, his hair was unwashed, his wig permanently askew, his footwear scuffed and scratched, his stockings always at half mast. He shaved when he was reminded to do so, which was not often for he lived alone and most preferred to keep a distance from the ripe aroma of his bodily presence. He shaved in the tiniest of mirrors, one sufficient to see a dozen or so bristles at a time.

However, all this was to change on his meeting a woman with whom he believed he would like to create a line of fine descendants.

It was his time to marry, he had decided.

His courting excursions settled on a petite neatly dressed affectionate young woman. In this case, an opposite surely attracted its own opposite and they wed, to the wonder of many.

For all their differences, none could have been happier than the newly weds appeared to be.

The only impediment to complete harmony was the uncouth and slovenly appearance of the bride's loving giant of a husband, though both appeared to be deliriously happy, none more so than the bridegroom who carried himself through the streets of Dublin as the most fortunate of men.

His wife's name is lost to time; she was known as none other than the wife of Mr Conaty; but she will be known in this narrative as Eleanor, for we must address her as something other than an appendage of a wealthy man.

It was Eleanor who caused her husband to almost lose his reason when confronted by his own self, strange as that might seem.

The couple lived in a fine Georgian house in the centre of Dublin within a comfortable walk of the Four Courts. It was the property of Mr Conaty before he married.

It was purchased with the proceeds of his courtly duties and furnished in as haphazard a way as was his personal attire. A number of servants kept the house in as mannerly a state as they could, though it was not easy serving a man as capricious as Mr Conaty in his living habits.

Assuming her position as homemaker, Eleanor straightaway engaged extra domestic staff to begin unwinding years of neglect and preparing for the anticipated years of bonhomie to come.

Her new husband did not seem to notice the transformation going on around him. In time, Eleanor came to realise that her husband was quite simply incorrigible.

No matter how she dressed him in the morning as a well-tended married man, he returned of an evening as a single man who had lived in a primeval state for many years.

Though words were his stock-in-trade, neither entreaty nor cajolement had any effect on him.

To remedy this; on one fine day, in July, she determined she would show him to himself as others saw him. He would be surprised, of that she had no doubt. Once apprised of the situation, he would surely change his ways, and be grateful to her for showing him the way.

Of such follies are the path of early married life strewn.

Eleanor, on first coming into her new estate, had studied the gloomy hall and had determined that visitors to her home would see a well-furbished entrance. The high entrance hall of the house they lived in was transformed into a welcoming space.

The staircase in such grand houses in Dublin were well set back from the hall door and did not intrude on the consciousness of the newly-arrived. Visitors were free to step into a ground floor room, or, to continue downwards to the basement where lay the kitchens.

It was in this entrance space that Eleanor had a very tall mirror placed, facing the street door.

A leading firm of mirror makers attached the pier-glass to the wall and angled it so that anyone stepping in from the world outside would see their own reflection in the mirror.

It would be a special feature of this house, for such mirrors were usually installed between the full-length windows of houses of the period, the better to reflect daylight and to give a sense of splendour to all parts of the room in question and to the entire house by extension.

In this case, arriving gentlemen could approve of their appearance in the mirror before stepping in to the company. Ladies could ensure they were of their best appearance, allowing for any last minute adjustments to style.

Everyone would be pleased, Eleanor assured herself, happily.

She very much wanted this to be. She loved Mr Conaty more than she ever believed possible. In her sleep she could see his deep dark eyes ravishing every part of her; in daylight she attended to his every movement. She listened for his key in the door each evening with a breath-catching anticipation she had not even dreamt of in her maiden days.

Her pleasure would be complete if only he would match his personal appearance with her vision for him.

An unconcerned Mr Conaty had never seen more than his chin or part of his neck reflected in his tiny shaving mirror. If he had ever seen all of his full reflection at once, as others saw him, he seemed to have not registered any discomfort, nor any memory of it.

With that in mind, Eleanor truly believed that when he saw the fright he outwardly was to others, he would surely mend his ways.

However, in hindsight she came to believe that with a little more foresight she might have anticipated what might happen when a man was confronted with the reality of his outward appearance while he was pre-occupied with how he might argue a legal point on the morrow.

In which case, Eleanor might have taken the precaution to tell him what she had done, and to ask his opinion of his appearance, once he had met his full reflection.

Since their marriage, she had come to recognise the inner beauty of the man she now called husband. It was time for the world to see him as he truly was.

She stood ready to assure him that he was not a lost cause and that with some tiny suggestions from her and his many friends and well-wishers he would reveal the magnificent man he was to an approving world.

All this she rehearsed in her mind. All this she saw as a drawing-room play with herself as heroine saving her beloved husband from himself.

However, in none of her imaginings did she foresee what did happen when Mr Conaty stepped in to the sanctuary of his own home.

He spied his loving wife standing at the foot of the stairs in that lime green dress that was his favourite. Her well-rehearsed hand rested on the lower banister in a position of casual welcome and enticement she had practised over many days.

Somewhere in her reflections on this moment had been a re-enactment of the fairytale of beauty and the beast where Mr Conaty the beast would finally realise how wonderful his wife appeared, even in her own carefully-selected informal home attire, and how rough and unkempt he himself appeared to others.

He would immediately change his ways, be grateful to her for many years, and their love would intensify, if that was even possible.

She took a breath when the heavy wooden door swung open on its well-oiled hinges. He was here. The moment of truth was upon them.

Like many a bride before her, Eleanor was to be astonished by the response of her husband to her initiative.

Sadly, it was the opposite of what she had planned, for her husband soon sprang into action.

Mr Conaty had faced down formidable foes in court and emerged victorious from most of his battles. However, this was different, this was his home and it threatened the safety of his good wife.

For, Mr Conaty, never having seen himself in full regalia, did not know who the man was staring back at him from the mirror in his own home.

He saw only a hostile savage poised to leap forward. When he moved, the savage advanced in a very similar manner. Mr Conaty uttered a loud cry, and struck the approaching beast several blows with his walking stick. He was oblivious to glass shattering everywhere about him. In his excitement he toppled over and fell on the ground, where he anticipated the blows of his adversary upon his defenceless body.

The noise roused several servants with some alacrity for all had been aware of the trust Eleanor placed in the mirror to change their life for good. They picked their master up and laid him gently on a long sofa in the drawing room.

A doctor was sent for who proceeded to bleed the patient to bring him back to his senses, as was the custom of the day.

People fussed about the felled lawyer until he was taken up to his bedroom to recover in private.

Physical recovery was swift; but it was no easy matter to banish from his mind the memory of the horrible figure that had threatened him in his hallway.

Some thought it wisest to say it was not a monster in flesh and blood, but the devil himself whom Mr Conaty had bested in his mortal struggle to save his beloved wife.

As for Eleanor, she quietly arranged for the shards of the offending mirror to be removed from their life for she loved Mr Conaty far too much to ask him to do battle with the devil, for a second time, just to look nice for her.

And as far as is know the real-life beauty and the beast lived in quite contentment well into old age without the use of a single mirror in the hall ever again.

28

An island love

Great love stories are often those of a love unfulfilled. Cáit Daly did not marry anyone, yet when she died, the waters between the Great Blasket Island and the mainland were filled with boats full of mourners who escorted her remains to the mainland for burial, on a broiling hot summer's day.

This love story happened off the south-west coast, and featured someone more noted for telling the story of his people than the story of his own love life.

In *The Islandman* Tomás Ó Criomhthain (Tomás O'Crohan in English) chronicled the history of his fellow islanders on the Great Blasket Island.

He loved Cáit Daly from the neighbouring island of Inisvickillane, yet he married another woman with whom he had a large family.

The young Tomás often went to Inisvickillane to be in the company of the Daly family.

On that island, nature provided a multitude of rabbits, and birds and eggs aplenty. Man provided sheep, and cows to produce milk and butter that were consumed by those who lived on Inisvickillane and their guests.

For Tomás, the other island became a fabled place. There was sport and fun and company of his own age there with fine lively girls with big hearts that paid him much attention when he was among them.

It was not long before Cáit, the eldest girl of the family but who was four years younger than Tomás and who had attended the primary school on the Great Blasket at the same time as he, began to pay him more attention. He was very pleased at this turn of events.

Tomás described Cáit as a fine nice girl; the finest singer around, which was an effusive comment for a young man of that place and time. Both could sing the songs that spoke of love and tragedy and they sang them together.

Other Great Blasket islanders travelled to Inisvickillane in search of rabbits. They also took gulls' eggs and killed seals for food and profit. But for Tomás the island held just one interest and that was Cáit and her laughing eyes and lovely singing voice. His interest was reciprocated by the singing girl. He and Cáit were happy then and the world belonged to them. The Islandman was to say it became his soul's desire to marry her, and to spend the rest of his days with her.

One way to accomplish that was to become a *cliamhain isteach* to her family on their island. Such a man married and moved in with his wife's birth family to become a part of that household and to support the old couple, the parents, in their declining years.

The prospect of moving to Inisvickillane to live with Cáit in peace and love was an attractive one. The brothers of Cáit would leave for America in their own time and there would be need for a man about the house, then. Tomás described Cáit and her sisters as well-formed young women, bright-skinned, with fair or golden hair, running the happy family home between them. Life was good on Inisvickillane for him, according to the writings Tomás left behind for us to read about those halcyon years.

Their relationship moved closer when on one fine evening Cáit left the company and stepped elegantly and slowly through the open doorway of the cottage they were all gathered in. Tomás saw her wave to him, that he might follow. He did so.

Not pretending anything at all to the company other than he was stepping outside, he was unsurprised to find she had not gone far from the house, but was waiting for him in the shadows.

He joined her in the soft darkness with the sound of the rolling Atlantic Ocean in their welcoming ears and love in their eyes and hearts.

On another visit on a different day and in daylight they went a little way from the house, walking as slowly as two people ever did who never want to reach their destination.

Cáit came to a halt on a grassy hill while Tomás waited for her, wondering all the while what she was about. He saw her lean over to get at something on the ground. His breath caught in his throat at the beauty of her leaning form. While Tomás was so transported with young love's dream, Cáit drew from beneath a flat stone two fine rabbits that were hidden there. She had chosen them the previous day as being the best from a dozen caught then. They were for him, she said.

Such consideration convinced Tomás that she was the girl for him, and not only for him, but for his parents back at home in his own house on his own island. Instead of going to her island they would live on his island and make their future there, he decided.

With that single thought their story spun from love to tragedy. If storm clouds gathered above them they failed to see them at all.

On returning to his own Great Blasket Island, Tomás made known to his uncle, Diarmaid Ó Sé, his mother's brother, that he would like to marry Cáit Daly from Inisvickillane, if Diarmaid would act for him to arrange the marriage.

Diarmaid straightaway began to work on the parents of Tomás pointing out that they were growing older and it was time there was someone in around the house to offer them assistance or help.

In one year, two at the most, they would need a livelier person to see to the daily responsibilities of the household.

But, the haphazard Diarmaid only did half a job of it. He said he had a message for the old couple from the finest girl who ever walked, who was the best and finest in every way. By which he meant he had someone in mind to marry Tomás. But, he said no more that that, for he believed the issue settled with his words, whatever Cáit or Tomás would make of it.

Such matters could not be left to chance, for there was no state pension or assistance to older people to help them survive, in those years. In the island tradition younger people took over the running of a household, taking care of the older people, as a duty that came with the house.

In this case, an intervention came from a third party that while practical was to cause heartache in many lives. The nub of it was that both of them had ageing parents that needed taking care of in the years that were to follow. That they lived on different islands complicated matters.

Tomás was the youngest in his family, the shirtail. His eldest sister, Máire, went to America when she was widowed. She returned after some time and remarried and now lived on the island.

It was she who took a hand when she heard Diarmaid was matchmaking between Cáit Daly from Inisvickillane and her little brother Tomás. She spelt out to the old couple the obligation that the incoming person would have. There was a conflict between the future of both families on different islands, she said.

She did not leave it at that but said she herself had a good, well-meaning girl in mind for her parents' older years, who had her own people nearby in the village on the Great Blasket who could help in time of need, if Tomás would marry her instead.

She did not let it lie until she had the agreement of the old couple, and Tomás himself, to his marriage to Máire Ni Chathain (Máire Keane in English).

There were certain times in the calendar year when people could not wed in church; so the days before or after that date were popular for marriages. One such day was close at hand when Máire the sister laid down the law for all of them.

That is how it happened that one week from that day Tomás O'Crohan and Máire Keane were married on Shrove Tuesday, 5th February 1878 in Ballyferriter church on the mainland, for there was no church on the islands.

When the couple was declared married in the eyes of God by the officiating priest, they departed for the Great Blasket having supped a little in the local public house beforehand. Neighbours gathered into the house for a hooley that reached on into the next day day's dawning. Families came from nearby islands to celebrate an island wedding.

Among them were people from Inisvickillane, including Cáit, according to an account given by Mícheál Ó Dubhshláine in his 2009 book *Inisvickillane*.

When it came time for the groom to sing, Tomás sang *The Dark Woman from the Mountain*. It is a sad, lonely song, full of sorrow from a girl whom her boy has forsaken, and broken her heart in the doing of it.

It was the only song he sang at his wedding. Whether it was a duty song or a message to Cáit only he could say and we will never know for sure.

Tomás and Máire settled down to have a large family --- ten in all between boys and girls, many of whom died one way or another before their father.

Tomás departed this world in 1937, aged 81 years. Maire passed away in June 1904, in childbirth. Tomás said on her passing that it was then that he was really left blind.

Tomás was 21 years of age on the day of his wedding, which would suggest Cáit was 17 years old at that time.

That Cáit did not remain much longer on Inisvickillane. Like most of her brothers and sisters, she went to America to better her circumstances. She returned four or five years later from the failed experiment for her that was America. She did not marry there, nor, at home either.

There would be no going away again for her, for she died on Inisvickillane in June 1885, aged 24 years. Her health had failed dramatically when she contracted tuberculosis.

Her father and brothers made a coffin for her from driftwood washed in on the tide to their island. She was waked in her own home, where she had been courted by the handsome Tomás O'Crohan.

Her remains were taken by boat on a calm day to the Great Blasket Island and thence to Dunquin for burial.

Eighteen naomhóg canoes crossed together, cutting through the sea in one long line as the funeral cortege crossed the four of five kilometres of water to the last resting place of a lost love.

Tomás O'Crohan was in one of the naomhóg canoes quietly paying his private respects to the memory of a lost love.

29

Gold of the heart

Cáit and Sean saw the man approach their hillside farm long before he knew it was there. Their cottage rested between two large rocks in a fold of land. The only trace of its existence from afar was a thin trail of smoke from a turf fire in the hearth.

They had not always been poor. When they were young and in their first blush of almost-married love Cáit inherited the land on the passing away of her parents. They were childhood sweethearts and it was natural they should marry.

In companionship, they tried to create their Garden of Eden. They tried. And tried. And for a while they succeeded but a run of bad summers and poor prices for their produce sapped their energy and their reserves. Their will faltered a little and faded over some advancing years until the farm was now in the poor condition the stranger saw from the road.

Fences sagged out of line as far as his eye could see on the twisting turning road where grass grew in the middle of the little-used thoroughfare.

A sad staring cow appeared listless to the point of apathy. The ground beneath her feet was worn away to dust from overuse. A black goat seemed not to care whether it walked or sat down. A mountain collie barked more from memory that any real intention to raise an alarm.

The man paused at the gate to study the silent house. Fresh paint had not covered the rusted gate in years. It screeched loudly when he pushed at it with a firm hand to gain access to the yard.

He moved some unresisting sheep out of his way with his knees without breaking stride in his crossing of the yard.

On the roof, hens sat in hollows pecked into the thatch. Holes so created allowed rain to drip onto the clay floor, turning it into soft yielding squelching mud.

No glass graced a pair of foot-square windows that used to dress the front of the building. Instead, kidskins were stretched across crooked sticks to deny access to creeping cold winds. Very few sods of turf were stacked at the gable against the winter to come.

Even the peeling wooden door inside the storm porch craved attention. Picking a clear spot among the curling shards of dry wood the stranger rapped on the door with his knuckles and awaited a response.

Long ago, it was common for people to walk the roads of Ireland without shelter or home to call their own. Some were dispossessed by the Great Famine of the 19th century and the cholera epidemic that followed the catastrophic potato crop failure. More outgrew large families on smallholdings when space ran out for everyone to live together. These individuals struck out on their own to walk the endless roads seeking opportunity and fortune. Some were travelling tradespeople always moving on to new clients who had no means of transport to come to them.

Some seemed to come from nowhere and to go on to nowhere, turning away questions or greetings from all they met. Most however carried stories and news with them. In this place and that, they gathered news from their hosts to carry on to the next place.

The door opened to the patient stranger. That its hinges protested without adequate lubrication easing their way came as no surprise to the caller.

After the man had blessed all inside as was the way of the times, Sean bade him welcome. It was the custom to render hospitality to those travelling the roads, be that food or a bed for the night.

Allowing that the person was presentable and tidy they would be lodged in the house. If they had not been in the presence of cleansing water, or, soap in living memory they were housed in the barn with any smoking pipes they might have being taken from them.

Too many careless tramps had fallen asleep while smoking a final pipe of the evening for farmers to take any chances with sudden and excited conflagration and a disappeared guest.

Cáit cleaned her hand in her apron before rising to offer greeting to the stranger. They bade him sit by the fire on the little wooden form that would take two people, or three at a pinch. With a wooden spoon Cáit stirred the bubbling pot of stew that hung on a blackened crane over the smoking fire. With a large dipping mug she extracted enough for all three of them. Their visitor saw the bottom of the old pot and knew they had shared tomorrow's meal with him, for such stewings were made for several days consumption.

Their conversation and chat went on until darkness surrounded the little house. Sean lit a candle then and placed it on the wooden mantelpiece and for a while the flickering shadows played on their gathered faces before it settled down to a steady flame.

They made up a settle bed by the fire for him. They gave him the good blanket that Cáit kept in a hope chest in the corner.

For pillow, he folded his top coat carefully beneath his head so no button would meet his sleeping face.

Sean and Cáit had arrived at the middle part of their lives now and did not care to stay up past sleeping time, even though they might have a visitor. There was always the morning for more chat.

For signal Cáit went into the room after saying a soft goodnight while Sean doused the candle above the fireplace, though there was light enough to see yet by the fire's embers.

The stranger slept until dawn when a rooster declared that yet another weary day had begun. He slept longer than his hosts who were up and about before him. Sean had been to the well and brought back water, by then; Cáit had the grate cleared and new firing placed on top of the embers, a pot was bubbling away with three fresh eggs sitting neatly inside the tumbling water.

Cáit cleared away the table and placed a round cake of griddle bread at the stranger's disposal. Beside it was a pat of butter she had made herself. Sean brewed a large pot of tea. He strained the tea leaves through the strainer and moved a bag of white sugar with a spoon in it before their guest to sweeten his tea to taste.

They chatted some more about people the stranger had met until it came time for him to leave. He shook out his coat and put it on. He picked up his walking stick and swung his bag across his shoulder.

He was ready to leave, but before he stepped away from the house, he reached deep down into the bag. Sean hurriedly restrained his hand for he believed the stranger meant to offer to pay. This they could not accept.

Nonetheless, their guest drew a piece of soft cloth from his bag. They wondered at it for they could see it covered something else.

He handed it gently to Cáit and said it was for their welcome to him and the hospitality they had offered to him a stranger whom they did not know.

It was little enough; but, he hoped he would be welcome here when next his journey took him along this way.

He asked them not to open the cloth until he was away down the road. Neither Cáit nor Sean knew what to say in response.

Before they could decide which of them should speak, the stranger had opened the squeaking door and was away across the yard and through the road gate in a few strides. He was gone before the dog could rise up from the ground to bark even once.

Wondering what on earth he could have given them as a gift, Cáit unwrapped the cloth and there in the palm of her hand was a small bar of gold.

Neither of them had ever seen an object of such value before; much less held it in their hands. Sean ran to call the stranger back. But the road was empty in all directions, search as he might.

He returned to the house to meet his wife who was in a fearful state. She said it was too much for such a poor family. How were they to explain this if the police were to ask where it came from?

Never minding the police or anyone else and setting aside such considerations, Sean wrapped the gold bar carefully in the cloth after scrutinising it in silence for a moment of time. In the bedroom was a loose stone in the wall behind their bed that offered a secure hiding place. He said they needed time to consider what to do. In the meantime, there was no need to tell anyone what fortune had visited them in this house on this day.

Cáit agreed on this course with Sean even if she still feared the day when she might have to explain how they came to have this gold in their possession.

Sean made it his business to ask everyone he could think of that lived or moved through the townland if they had seen the stranger. No one could say they had.

A great many days followed that one, in turn, until enough dawns had gathered to mark a full year on the village grocer's complimentary calendar hanging from a nail on the kitchen wall.

The wind blew dust along the road just as it had done a year ago, and as it would for many more years to come. Much was unchanged in the landscape when the stranger's footsteps moved along the road, once more.

He saw that the fence was fixed, its lines running straight and true now. The cow was moved to where grass grew in abundance; the goat was shaking itself in apparent contentment. From the road, he could see no hens roosting on the newly thatched roof. The gate swung silently to his touch, the dog ran forward, tail wagging at a familiar friend. There was glass in the windows, the house was newly whitewashed and strong smoke rose from the chimney. The front door was newly painted a decisive red.

He tapped lightly on the soft wood.

That he received a hero's welcome from Cáit and Sean would be to understate the occassion.

They took his coat, they placed more fuel on the fire, used the bellows to rise the flame. They made him a meal of mutton, potatoes and cabbage that he knew came from their own stock. The floor was no longer damp and slippery underfoot. There was new sand scattered across the ground to keep it clean and dry.

They spoke excitedly of their plans for the next year and extracted a solemn promise from him that he would mark this date with an annual visit. They fell silent then for when a couple has lived together for many years it is often not necessary to speak aloud. Whatever passed between them, Cáit arose and went into the bedroom, to return holding the cloth the stranger had left with her a year before.

Sean stood beside her with his arm around her waist, as he had done in their first years of life together. Cáit unwrapped the gold bar. She held it out to the stranger, smiling.

She said: "You left this here a year ago, we want you to take it and carry it to someone else that needs it."

The stranger said he did not understand how everything was so improved and yet the gold bar was untouched?

Sean said they had hidden the gold bar in a safe place until they should need it. However, in the interim they realised they had some chicken wire and a few lengths of timber lying about the place. He made a hen house and a run for the fowl to stay within and off the roof where their eggs were often lost in the thatch or fell through to break on the floor below. Eggs collected by Cáit from the hen house were sold by her in the market.

They purchased more fencing and moved the livestock to where grass grew stronger. They prospered. They had enough money for a visit to the bull with the cow. The cow had a calf that they kept for future profit.

Goat's milk they sold also and with all the milk they had they made butter. Cáit sold butter with her eggs.

Then there were enough funds left over to paint the place, whitewash the cottage and repair the windows.

Whenever a dark day came --- and there were a few of them in the beginning --- they took the gold bar out, placed it on the blanket and looked at it before putting it back in its safe keeping.

They asked their visitor to take the gold bar with him, for while their gold bar was in their hearts, they had no need of anything else.

30

Love potions and other lures

Love between two people can be affected by outside influences in the form of potions and lures and piseógs, or, superstitions. Whether you believe these or not, it is well to be informed so as to make your wisest decision in the matter of love.

Some of the country people have memory of very powerful herbal remedies, while love potions are even now still in use in places. They are generally prepared by an old woman; but must be administered by the person who wishes to inspire the tender passion, or they will not work.

For example: a fine, handsome young man of the best character and conduct suddenly became wild and reckless, drunken and disorderly, from the effect, it was believed, of a love potion administered to him by a young woman who was passionately in love with him.

Conversely, when she saw the change produced in him by her act, she became moody and nervous herself, as if a constant terror was over her.

No one ever saw her smile again. She became half deranged and after a few years of a strange, solitary, life she died of melancholy and despair; which hardly seemed fair to anyone.

What happened to the gentleman in this case we cannot say for our attention is on lures that people use and their consequences for their user.

Lady Wilde, the mother of Irish playwright Oscar Wilde, and a collector of stories in her own right in the 19th century, reported on a charm that no mortal woman may resist. It concerned a paper on which words of import were written.

Viz: the paper, on being opened, was found to contain five mysterious words written in blood, and in this order

Sator.

Arepo.

Tenet.

Opera.

Rotas.

These letters are so arranged that read in any way, right to left, left to right, up or down, the same words are produced; and when written in blood with a pen made of an eagle's feather, they form a charm which no woman can resist. If there be any doubt as to the veracity of this lure then the incredulous reader can easily test the truth of this assertion, by trying it out on a suitable recipient, said a paper of the time.

If for some reason it does not do as expected then the liver of a thoroughly black cat is sovereign in the process of procuring a return of love.

At least it was at one time in the County Wexford.

Nora, a healthy bouncing country maiden who was in no way gifted with outstanding natural beauty vowed she would be the wife of young Mr. Bligh, a half sir who lived not far away.

Aided by her sister and another woman, Nora slew an unwilling and entirely innocent cat in the cause. The liver was carefully taken out, broiled, and reduced to a powder, according to Patrick Kennedy from Bunclody who made a study of the story.

Nora managed to get her man into her house and to accept a cup of tea with the cat's powder dissolved in it. By the time he took up his hat to walk home, he was lost in love. However, for the spell to work required the level of cat's tea in his system to be constantly topped up.

It took a crowd of his friends breaking into Nora's house the night before the marriage to carry him off to a secret location and to hold him incommunicado for a month without a drop of tea passing his lips to break the spell.

Another potent love-charm used by a certain type of woman is where a piece of skin that was taken from the arm of a corpse is tied on a sleeping person whose love is sought.

The skin is removed after some time, and carefully put away before the sleeper awakens or has any consciousness of the transaction.

As long as the strip of dead skin remains in the woman's possession the love of her beloved will be unchanged.

Otherwise, if a suitable sleeping quarry is not available, then the same strip of skin is placed under the pillow to dream on, in the name of the Evil One, when the future husband will appear in the dream, whether he is aware of it or not.

For men, a distaff was placed under the head of a young man at night to make him dream of the girl he was destined to marry.

This was mostly done in November, when the harvest was in and the coming winter provided for, and life was fairly relaxed.

A distaff is a staff for holding flax or wool in spinning which was usually undertaken by the women of a household.

Though in January, the girl who would wish to see her future husband must go and gather certain herbs in the light of the full moon of the new year, repeating this charm--

"Moon, moon, tell unto me
When my true love I shall see?
What fine clothes am I to wear?
How many children shall I bear?
For if my love comes not to me
Dark and dismal my life will be."

Then the girl cutting three pieces of clay from a sod with a black-hafted knife, carries them home, ties them into her left stocking with the right garter, places the parcel under her pillow, and dreams a true dream of the man she is to marry and her future fate.

Simple really.

Otherwise, ten leaves of hemlock dried and powdered and mixed in food or drink will make the person you desire love you in return.

When a person becomes low and depressed and careless about everything, they are said to have met a fairy blast.

Blast-water must be poured over them by the hands of a fairy doctor saying it is being done: "In the name of the saint with the sword, who has strength before God and stands at His right hand."

Whatever is left after the procedure must be poured on the fire.

Or, keep a sprig of mint in your hand till the herb grows moist and warm, then take hold of the hand of the woman you love, and she will follow you as long as the two hands close over the herb.

No invocation is necessary; but silence must be kept between the two parties for ten minutes, to give the charm time to work with due efficacy and ten minutes borrowed from eternity is not that much to set aside in any case.

But if ten minutes cannot pass in companionable silence between two people then there is no chance for such a liaison.

A charm of most desperate love, to be written with a raven's quill in the blood of the ring finger of the left hand by believers in divine intervention is:

"By the power that Christ brought from heaven, mayest thou love me, woman!

As the sun follows its course, mayest thou follow me.

As light to the eye, as bread to the hungry, as joy to the heart, may thy presence be with me,

O woman that I love, till death comes to part us asunder."

Or

Golden butter on a new-made dish to be given in the presence of a mill, of a stream, and the presence of a tree; the lover saying softly--

"O woman, loved by me, mayest thou give me thy heart, thy soul and body. AMEN."

There is one hour in every day when whatever you wish will be granted, but no one knows what that hour is. It is all a chance if we come on it when we are wishful.

Bonne chance.

Or

This is a charm I set for love; a woman's charm of love and desire; a charm of God that none can break-

"You for me, and I for thee and for none else; your face to mine, and your head turned away from all others."

This is to be repeated three times secretly, over a drink given to the one beloved.

Though whether you should offer a second drink if the first one does not work is not stated.

If a bride steers a boat on the day of her marriage, the winds and the waves have no power over it, be the tempest ever so fierce or the stream ever so rapid.

Fact.

In a traditional Irish wedding a beautiful new dress was presented to the bride by her husband at the marriage feast; at which also the father paid down her dowry before the assembled guests; and all the place around the house was lit by torches when night came on, and song and dance continued till daylight, with much speech-making and drinking of poteen.

If you are yet unmarried and to foresee happy days, take a piece of bride-cake and pass it three times through a wedding-ring, then sleep on it, and you will see in a dream the face of your future spouse.

The seed of docks tied to the left arm of a woman will prevent her being barren, so they say, but finding a likely man might be just as important.

Girls were warned to be especially careful in the first month of summer when Irish fairies, otherwise known as the Slua Sidhe, like to take away beautiful mortals to abide with them.

They famously took babies and left their own sickly offspring in their place: a changeling; but they also took away handsome adults and especially favoured a young woman on her wedding day.

One day in May, the first month of summer, a young girl lay down to rest at noontide on a fairy rath, or fort, and fell asleep. She should have known she was in great danger, for fairies are strong in power during the month of May and are particularly on the watch for a mortal bride to carry away to the fairy mansions, for they love the sight of human beauty.

The girl, though not yet a bride, went asleep in the human world and awoke in the Otherworld from which she never was known to return.

All of the above is fine; and you are urged to use caution and some discretion and personal responsibility should you choose to enter the world of lures and potions; but be aware that to some people to give a love potion is considered a very awful act, as the result may be fatal, or at least full of danger, either for the schemer or the victim and there is no arguing with that.

If you wish to go deeper into the dark side and to cause hatred between lovers take a handful of clay from a new-made grave, and shake it between them, saying: "Hate ye one another! May ye be as hateful to each other as sin to Christ, as bread eaten without blessing is to God."

An old man in Mayo, long ago, had great knowledge of charms, and of love philtres that no woman could resist.

Before his death he enclosed the written charms in a strong iron box, with directions that no one was to dare open it except the eldest son of an eldest son in a direct line from himself.

Whether such a man ever stepped forward we just do not know for the ways of love are mysterious and who can say with any certainty how two people fall in love and remain in that embrace for ever and ever.

But for sure love sustains and love endures for without love the world would be a sorrowful place.

May you fall in love and be filled with that intoxicating state that sends lovers into ecstasy beyond expectation.

May you know love in your life, for love is life itself.

And when you find love, tell it out.

Tell your story for we all live to hear it.

Be in love.

Be in love every moment of your life

for love

is life itself.

If you enjoyed this book why not order these other Brendan Nolan titles
http://brendannolan.ie/shop

Phoenix Park a History and Guidebook
This comprehensive guide is of interest to all lovers of this historic and scenic park. Now in an updated 2nd edition. ISBN 978-1-90830818-4

Barking Mad: Tales of Liars, Lovers, Loonies and layabouts
These tales of local characters he has met is a best-selling collection of stories Brendan has told on radio. ISBN 978-0-9560810-0-1

Dublin Folk Tales
These stories range from the strange to the profound, the tragic to the festive, from season to season and age to age. All are about Dubliners and their city, told by a Dublin storyteller. ISBN 978-1-845887285

Wexford Folk Tales
Wexford's rich heritage of myths and legends is uniquely captured in this collection of traditional tales from across the county. ISBN 978-1-845887667

Wicklow Folk Tales

Wicklow has as many stories as there are people travelling its roads; many are gathered here in this collection. Most of them are true

ISBN 978-1-845887858

The Little Book of Dublin

A reliable reference book and a quirky guide, this treasure trove can be dipped into time and time again to reveal something new about the people, the heritage and secrets of this ancient and fascinating city.

ISBN 978-1-845888152

Urban Legends of Dublin

Urban legends are the funny and frightening folklore people share today. Brendan explores Dublin's murky stories whispered in classrooms and backstreets. ISBN 978-1-845888602

Irish Love Stories CD

Irish Love Stories is storyteller Brendan Nolan and piper Martin Nolan performing Irish Love stories and tunes from our Celtic past.